TWISTED JOURNEYS® #14

ATTACK OF THE MUTANT METEORS

DAN JOLLEY

ILLUSTRATED BY DAVID WITT

GRAPHIC UNIVERSE™ · MINNEAPOLIS · NEW YORK

Story by Dan Jolley

Pencils and inks by David Witt

Coloring by Hi-Fi Design

Lettering by Marshall Dillon

Graphic Universe
A division of Lerner Publishing Group, Inc.
241 First Avenue North
Minneapolis, MN 55401 U.S.A.

Website address: www.lernerbooks.com

Library of Congress Cataloging-in-Publication Data

Jolley, Dan.
      Attack of the mutant meteors / by Dan Jolley ; illustrated by David Witt.
        p.   cm. — (Twisted journeys ; [#14])
      Summary: When two meteorites crash to Earth and open portals to fantastic
adventures, the reader must decide whether to take the path to a planet filled
with giant aliens or the gateway that offers the power to change one's size.
     ISBN: 978–0–8225–9249–5 (lib. bdg. : alk. paper)
     1. Plot-your-own stories. 2. Graphic novels. [1. Graphic novels.
2. Extraterrestrial beings—Fiction. 3. Size—Fiction. 4. Adventure and
adventurers—Fiction. 5. Science fiction. 6. Plot-your-own stories.]
    I. Witt, David, ill. II. Title.
PZ7.7.J65At 2010
741.5'973—dc22   2009020982

Manufactured in the United States of America
1 – DP – 12/15/2009

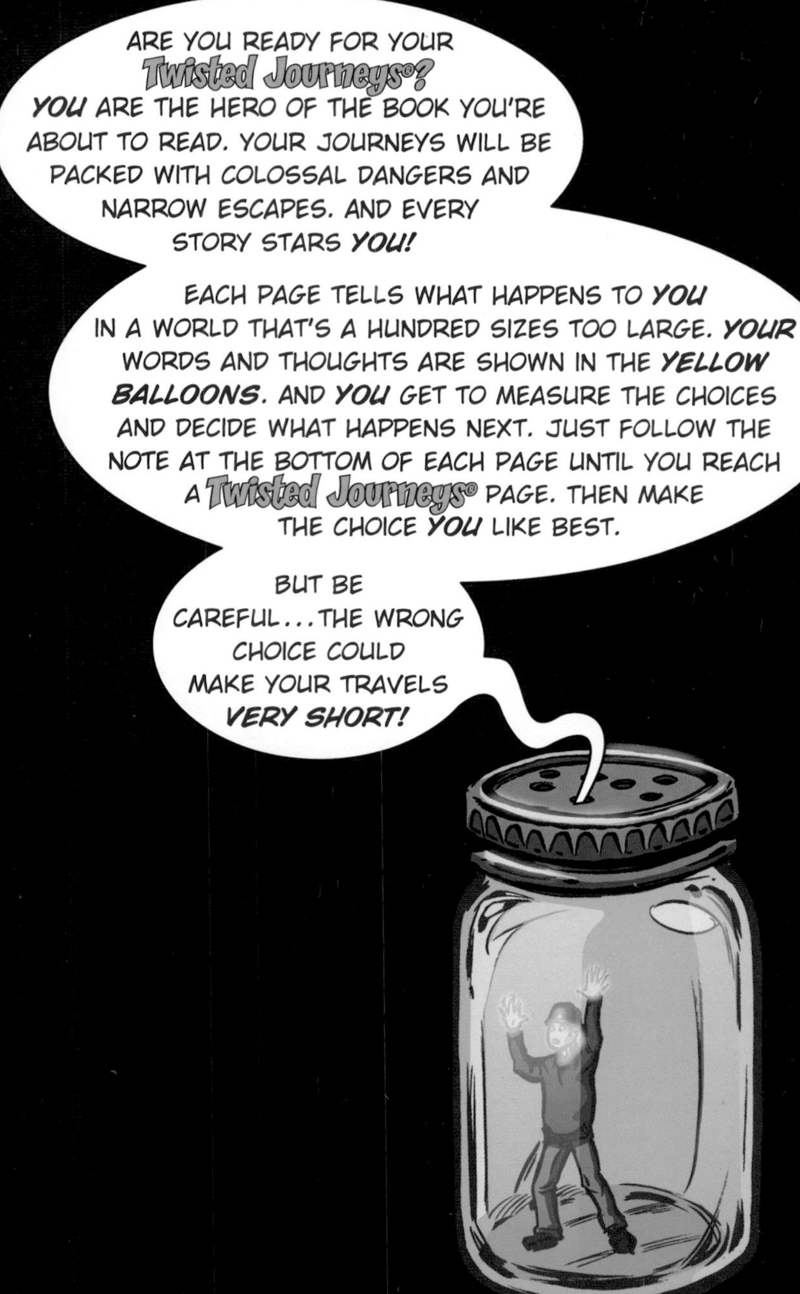
ARE YOU READY FOR YOUR Twisted Journeys®? YOU ARE THE HERO OF THE BOOK YOU'RE ABOUT TO READ. YOUR JOURNEYS WILL BE PACKED WITH COLOSSAL DANGERS AND NARROW ESCAPES. AND EVERY STORY STARS YOU!
EACH PAGE TELLS WHAT HAPPENS TO YOU IN A WORLD THAT'S A HUNDRED SIZES TOO LARGE. YOUR WORDS AND THOUGHTS ARE SHOWN IN THE YELLOW BALLOONS. AND YOU GET TO MEASURE THE CHOICES AND DECIDE WHAT HAPPENS NEXT. JUST FOLLOW THE NOTE AT THE BOTTOM OF EACH PAGE UNTIL YOU REACH A Twisted Journeys® PAGE. THEN MAKE THE CHOICE YOU LIKE BEST.
BUT BE CAREFUL . . . THE WRONG CHOICE COULD MAKE YOUR TRAVELS VERY SHORT!

"It's a beautiful day for going to the park! You just wish you didn't have to spend it hunting for insects.

"I don't see what's so great about insects anyway," your friend LeBron grumbles. You think he might be complaining because he hasn't been able to catch anything yet . . . but then, neither have you. Butterflies are *fast*, it turns out! LeBron complains, "Mr. Larrabee wouldn't make us do something like this."

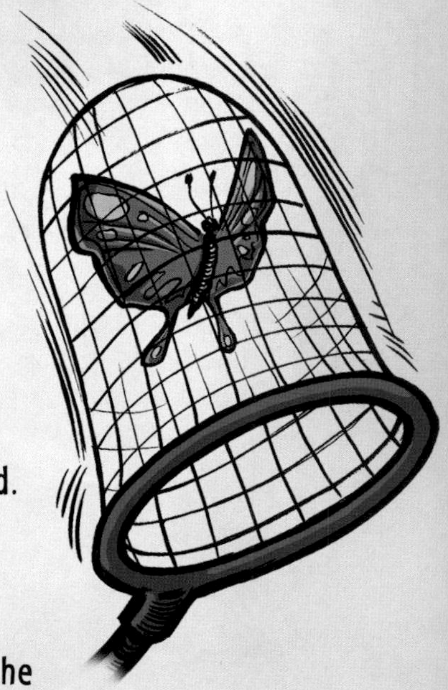

You tend to agree. You're only out here because your substitute teacher, Miss Fitch, seems to think insects are just the greatest things in the world. So you and the rest of your class had to pile onto the bus, come out to the park, and try your best to catch the tiny little creatures.

You're trying to think of something funny to say back to LeBron . . . when you notice something strange. "Hey." You point into the sky. "Look up there!"

GO ON TO THE NEXT PAGE.

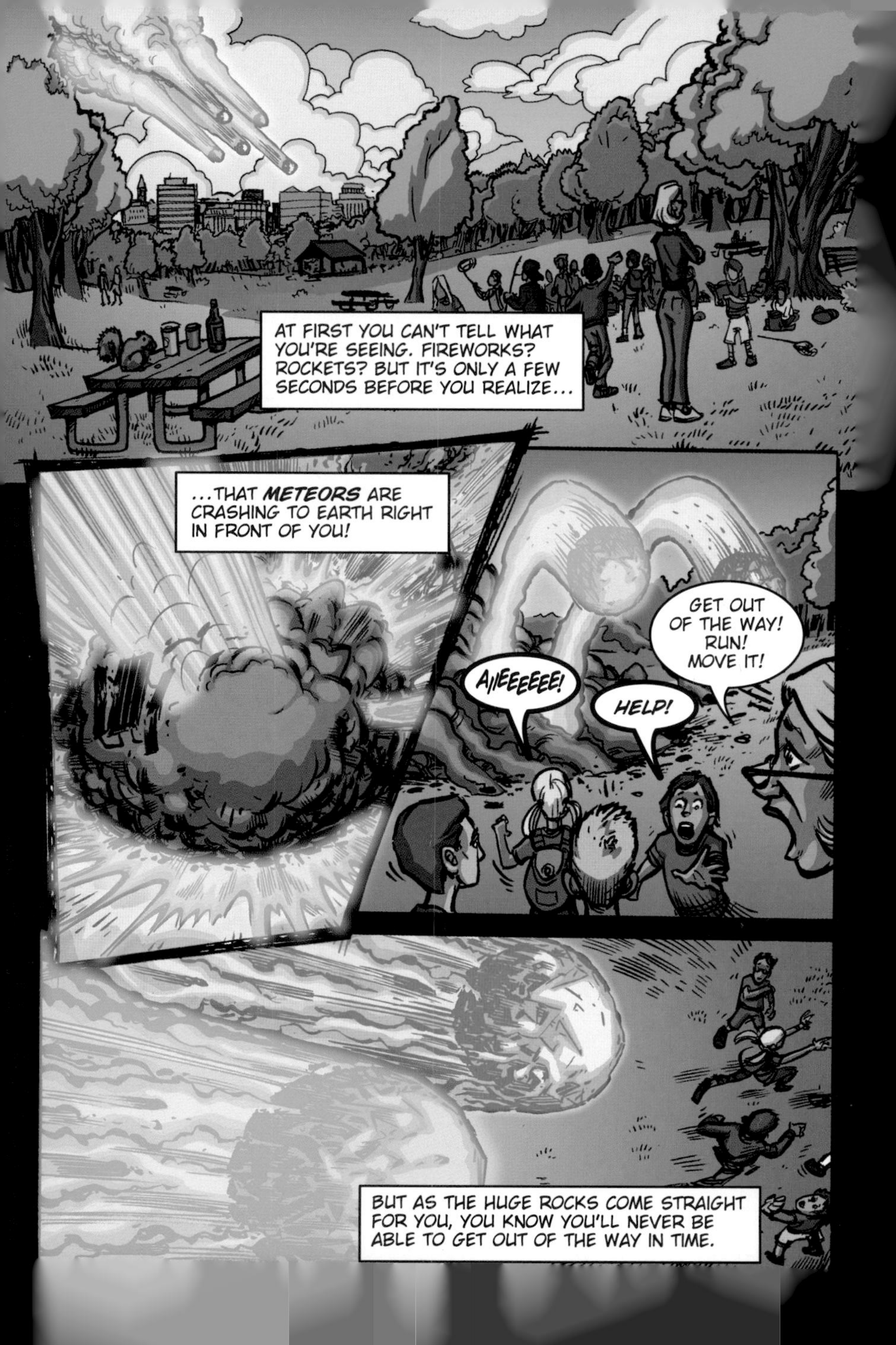
AT FIRST YOU CAN'T TELL WHAT YOU'RE SEEING. FIREWORKS? ROCKETS? BUT IT'S ONLY A FEW SECONDS BEFORE YOU REALIZE...
...THAT METEORS ARE CRASHING TO EARTH RIGHT IN FRONT OF YOU!
GET OUT OF THE WAY! RUN! MOVE IT!
AIIEEEEEE!
HELP!
BUT AS THE HUGE ROCKS COME STRAIGHT FOR YOU, YOU KNOW YOU'LL NEVER BE ABLE TO GET OUT OF THE WAY IN TIME.

The impact is so loud you think you've gone deaf for a second, and the ground shakes so hard it feels as if the earth itself has jumped up and punched you. Your brain really gets rattled for a moment . . .

. . . and then you open your eyes and realize you're *trapped*.

Two meteors have landed right on either side of you—two huge, glowing crystals stuck into the ground, with you right between them! You're wedged in so closely, the only way for you to get out from between these things is to climb over one of them.

You can hear the shouts of your classmates around you, but the only things you can see are the two crystals: one a brilliant green, the other a glowing yellow.

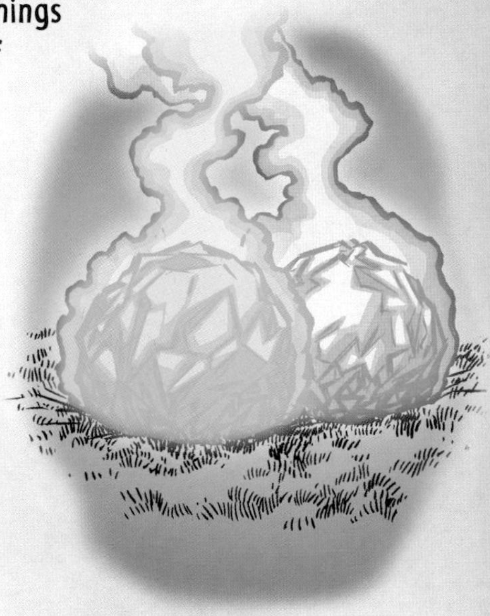

GO ON TO THE NEXT PAGE.

TWISTED JOURNEYS®

You can't just stay here—but you get a strange feeling from both of these huge crystals.

WILL YOU . . .

. . . climb over the green crystal?
TURN TO PAGE 18.

. . . tackle the yellow crystal?
TURN TO PAGE 66.

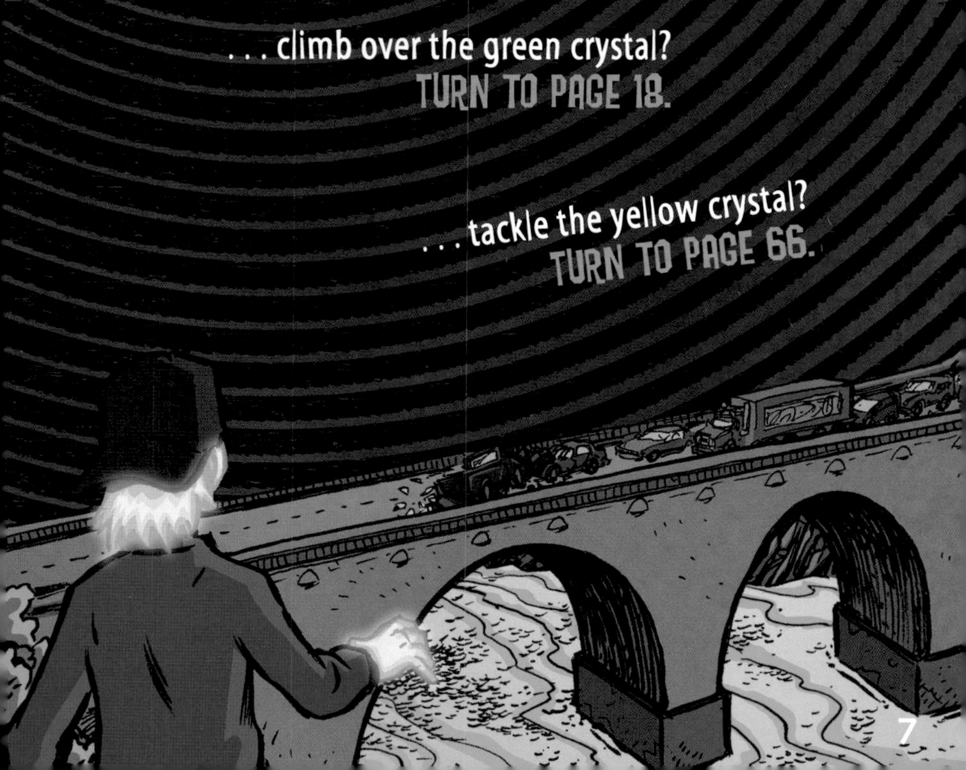

You open the metal door and go through—and then you realize that it wasn't a door at all. It was an access hatch to some sort of battery compartment.

"Look out!" Frummy shouts, spotting you. "I don't know how the batteries will react with your body's radiation!"

He was right to worry. Immediately the batteries start to pulse—and so does the glow around you! In a flash of white light, you disappear . . .

. . . and reappear in a completely different world! This one is all red, and strange things that look like shrimp float through the air.

Flash! It happens again! This time you're underwater, but you can still breathe.

Flash! Now you're on a purple mountaintop with little squids skittering around your feet.

Looks as if you're on a tour of the universe— permanently.

Flash!

THE END

The threat does sound pretty serious. But you're big enough to do whatever you want.

WILL YOU...

... agree to help get rid of the monster?
TURN TO PAGE 28.

... tell the commissioner, "Thanks, but no thanks"?
TURN TO PAGE 64.

... get a good look at that yellow crystal?
TURN TO PAGE 62.

Slowly and carefully, you start to climb up the door of the cat carrier. You move as quietly as you can too. You're pretty sure Miss Fitch wouldn't want you to monkey around with the cage.

It's hard to undo the latch at your new size! You have to hook one leg around one of the cage's bars and reach through with both hands to pop the catch. You think for a second Miss Fitch heard you . . .

. . . but you glance up and see that she's still giving the road all her attention, watching for street signs.

Swinging the bars open, you climb out and up onto the top of the carrier. From there it's not a huge jump to get over to the car door.

     TURN TO PAGE 14.

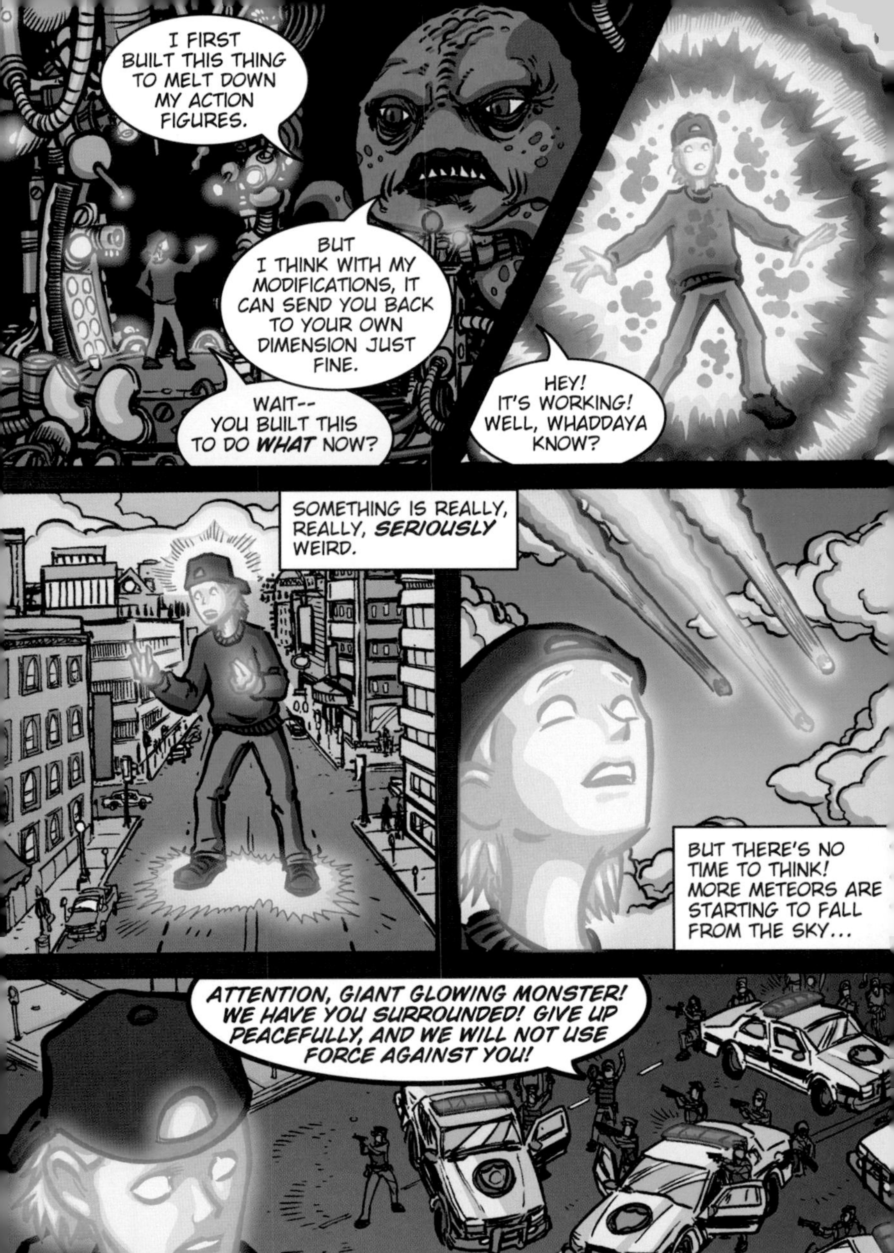

I FIRST BUILT THIS THING TO MELT DOWN MY ACTION FIGURES.
BUT I THINK WITH MY MODIFICATIONS, IT CAN SEND YOU BACK TO YOUR OWN DIMENSION JUST FINE.
WAIT-- YOU BUILT THIS TO DO **WHAT** NOW?
HEY! IT'S WORKING! WELL, WHADDAYA KNOW?
SOMETHING IS REALLY, REALLY, ***SERIOUSLY*** WEIRD.
BUT THERE'S NO TIME TO THINK! MORE METEORS ARE STARTING TO FALL FROM THE SKY...
ATTENTION, GIANT GLOWING MONSTER! WE HAVE YOU SURROUNDED! GIVE UP PEACEFULLY, AND WE WILL NOT USE FORCE AGAINST YOU!

The biggest of the bizarre giant children grabs you with a tentacle. "It's a pixie!" he says. "Hi, pixie! My name is Skurg."

Before you can say anything about not being a pixie, another kid bumps over to Skurg. "Let me see! Let me see!" she squeals. "Oooh, it's so cute! I wanna keep it! I wanna keep it!"

Skurg pulls you away from her. "Get lost, Kaurie! I found it! It's my pixie! An' I'm gonna play with it!"

"But I wanna take care of it!" Kaurie whines. "I'll take it home and feed it and give it nice things!"

"Forget it." Skurg seems very determined. "We're gonna play games and go on adventures and have lots of fun!"

"Well . . . maybe we should let the pixie decide," Kaurie says. She peers at you. "Who do you wanna go with? Me or Skurg?"

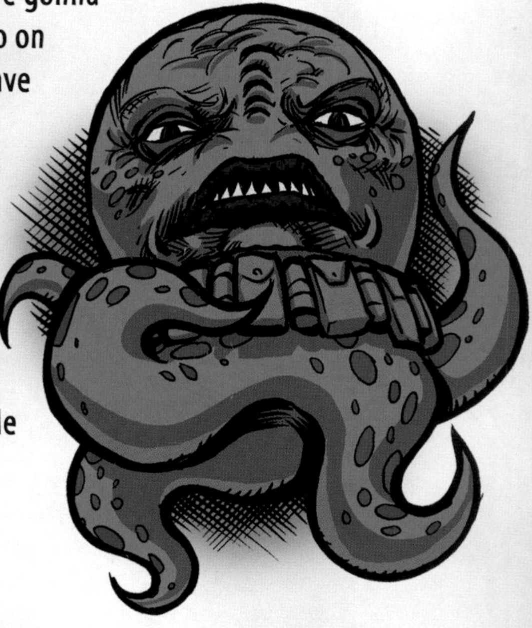

GO ON TO THE NEXT PAGE.

TWISTED JOURNEYS®

Despite how bizarre they look, playing with these kids might be fun. But you know you should be trying to get home.

WILL YOU...

. . . let Kaurie take you to her house?
TURN TO PAGE 30.

. . . go and hang out with Skurg?
TURN TO PAGE 51.

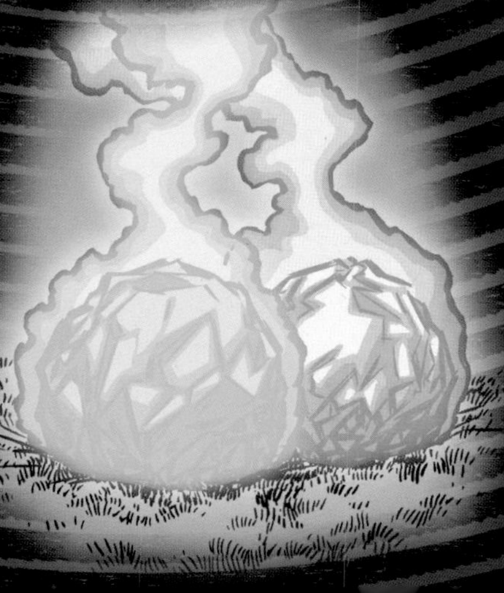

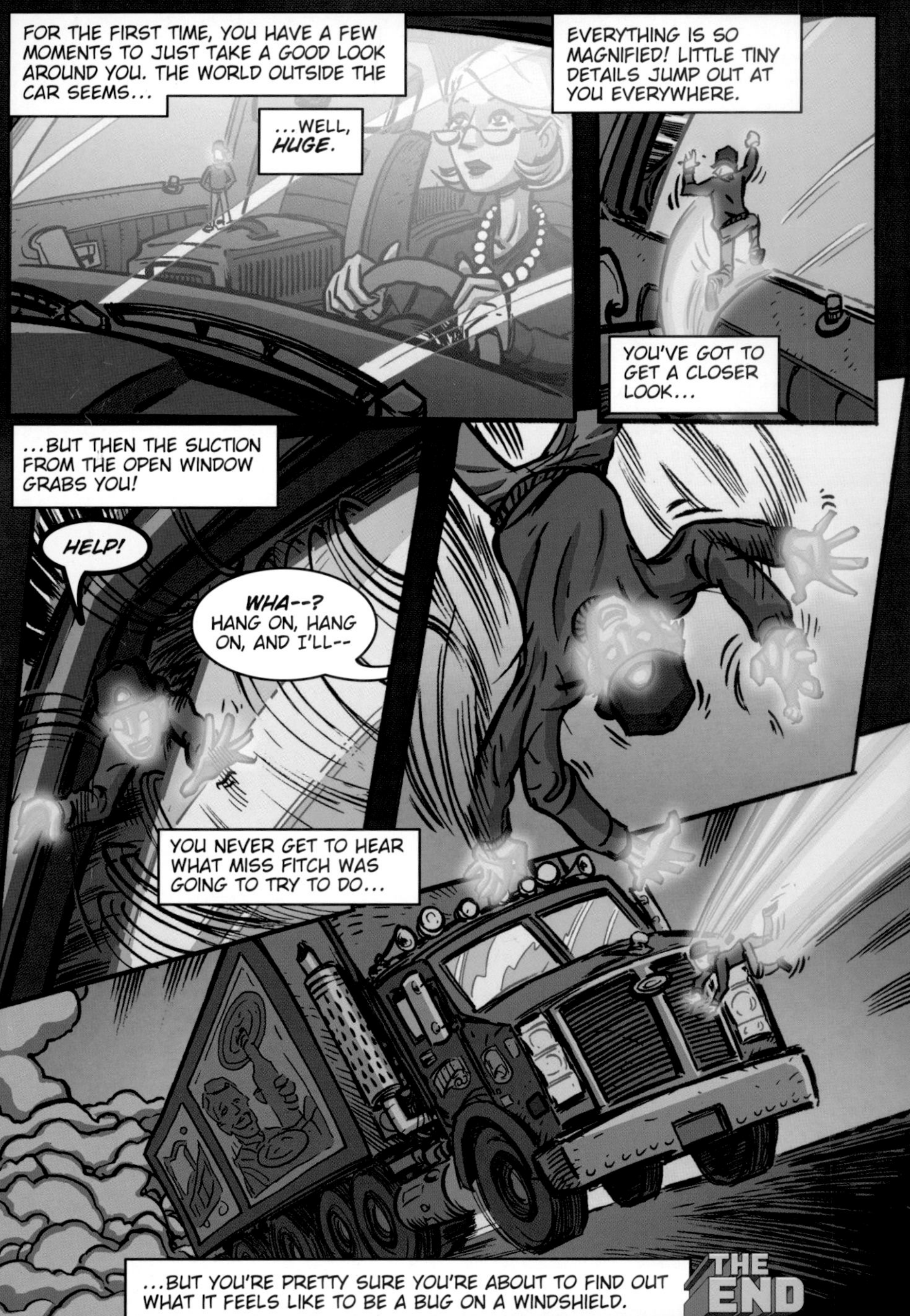
FOR THE FIRST TIME, YOU HAVE A FEW MOMENTS TO JUST TAKE A GOOD LOOK AROUND YOU. THE WORLD OUTSIDE THE CAR SEEMS...
...WELL, **HUGE.**
EVERYTHING IS SO MAGNIFIED! LITTLE TINY DETAILS JUMP OUT AT YOU EVERYWHERE.
YOU'VE GOT TO GET A CLOSER LOOK...
...BUT THEN THE SUCTION FROM THE OPEN WINDOW GRABS YOU!
HELP!
WHA--? HANG ON, HANG ON, AND I'LL--
YOU NEVER GET TO HEAR WHAT MISS FITCH WAS GOING TO TRY TO DO...
...BUT YOU'RE PRETTY SURE YOU'RE ABOUT TO FIND OUT WHAT IT FEELS LIKE TO BE A BUG ON A WINDSHIELD.
THE END

It's not a bad life, all things considered. The old lady's name is Akkatha, and she sets you up a very comfortable little living area in a huge, round bowl. Plus, the food she gives you tastes really good! You miss your family and your friends, but as the months and years go by, you actually start to think of this place as your home. Akkatha loves talking with you and takes excellent care of you. She doesn't seem to have any family. No one else ever comes to visit her.

Then one night, Akkatha hears about a big meteor shower on the way. "Would you like to go and see if we can find one of those?" she asks you gently. "It might be the same kind of stone that brought you here. You could get back to your home."

You look up into Akkatha's big, kind eyes. "Nah, that's all right," you tell her. "Maybe next time."

THE END

Who knows what kind of harebrained experiments this kid might perform on you? Too fast for him to notice, you scamper out the door of the tree house. Ordinarily you'd be stuck—but this tree is so huge, the bark is easy to climb down.

Once you get to the bottom, the cold, hard facts start hitting you: You're in some sort of alien dimension, filled with giant talking, floating aliens, giant blimplike vehicles floating overhead, and giant houses. Compared to the aliens, you're about half an inch tall. You figure wandering out into the wilderness on your own might not be the best plan.

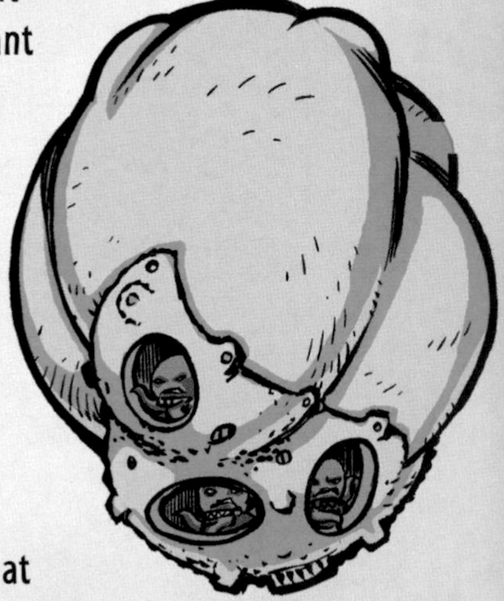

You have two choices that you can see:

One, go into Frummy's house, where maybe you could find something that would let you contact an adult.

Two, try to climb up to the huge, blimplike vehicle that's pausing near the roof of Frummy's house.

GO ON TO THE NEXT PAGE.

It probably won't be long before
Frummy comes looking for you.

WILL YOU...

... try to get inside his house?
TURN TO PAGE 21.

... climb on board the
yellow blimp?
TURN TO PAGE 106.

One crystal looks like as good a choice as the other, so you take a deep breath and jump up onto the green one. It's not as hard to do as you thought it would be. The crystal has a lot of cracks in it, so you can get good handholds and find places to wedge your toes in. It's not long before you're on top of it.

Your classmates are standing all around you, looking up at you with their mouths hanging open.

"What's the problem?" you ask. "I thought you guys would be happy to see I didn't get squished."

"Oh, we're happy," LeBron says. "But . . . you're *glowing*."

"Huh?" You look down at your hands—and he's right! You *are* glowing. You hop down to the ground . . .

. . . and the fall feels a lot farther than it should have, and the impact jars your legs.

Something's not right.

GO ON TO THE NEXT PAGE.

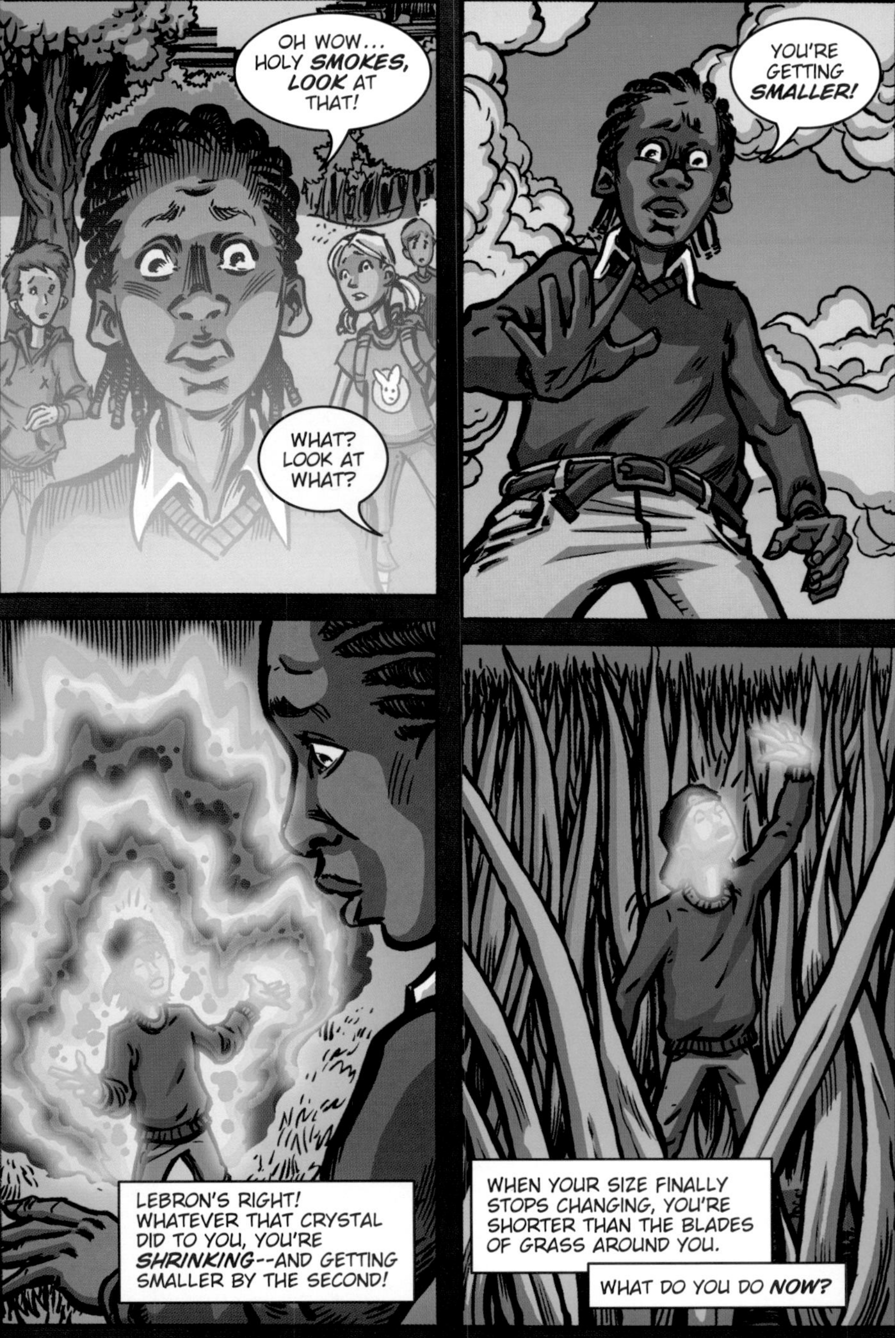
OH WOW... HOLY **SMOKES, LOOK** AT THAT!
WHAT? LOOK AT WHAT?
YOU'RE GETTING **SMALLER!**
LEBRON'S RIGHT! WHATEVER THAT CRYSTAL DID TO YOU, YOU'RE ***SHRINKING***--AND GETTING SMALLER BY THE SECOND!
WHEN YOUR SIZE FINALLY STOPS CHANGING, YOU'RE SHORTER THAN THE BLADES OF GRASS AROUND YOU.
WHAT DO YOU DO ***NOW?***

GO ON TO THE NEXT PAGE.

You could get stepped on at any second!

WILL YOU...

... try to run and find a safe place to hide?
TURN TO PAGE 42.

... yell for help and hope you can get someone's attention?
TURN TO PAGE 74.

Frummy's house is closed, but you're small enough to squeeze underneath it. You find yourself in a cavernous kitchen. At least, you *think* it's a kitchen. It's built for someone who can float and reach in every direction at once. Bizarre alien devices stick out from the walls, the floor, *and* the ceiling. You head for something that *could* be a telephone . . .

. . . but then you hear a growl that makes your breastbone vibrate. Stepping into the kitchen, its claws clicking on the floor, is a scale-covered creature the size of a school bus. It growls again and bares its teeth. You see a tag on the collar around its neck. It's a pet?

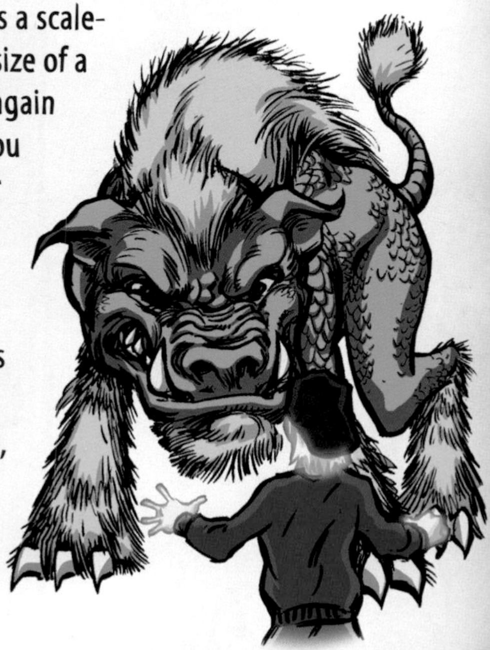

"N-n-nice doggie," you say, but it charges at you anyway. No matter where you run, it chases you. This thing could swallow you whole. There's only one place that's going to be safe from those teeth! You dodge its snapping jaws . . .

. . . and grab hold of its tag and swing up onto its head!

TURN TO PAGE 34.

You say good-bye to Miss Fitch and step into the special carrying case Major Green has for you. It's pretty neat, with a little chair just your size in it. "What do we do first?" you ask her.

"Well, first, we let you call your mother, so she won't worry," she says as she carries you down a long hallway. "Then we're going to try to get to the root of the problem."

"How're you going to do that?"

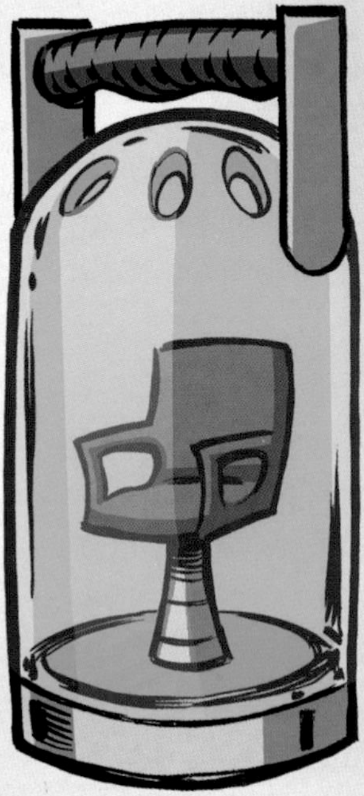

As you ask the question, she pushes open a big set of double doors. On the other side is an enormous room lined with lab equipment—and in the middle is the glowing green meteorite you touched, sealed inside a glass case. Lots of lab technicians scurry back and forth, performing tests.

"We're getting right to the heart of the matter," Green tells you. "We're studying the meteorite itself."

GO ON TO THE NEXT PAGE.

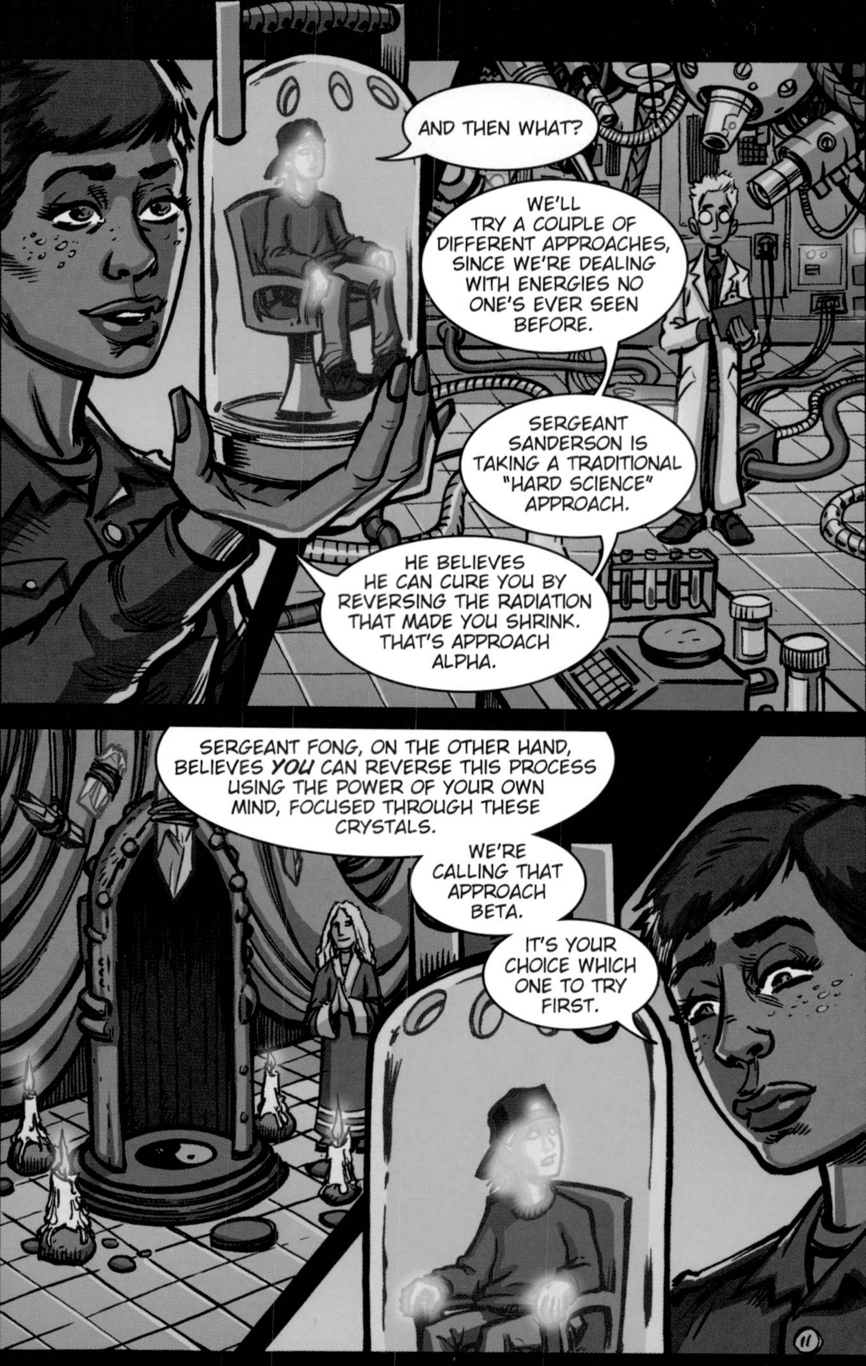
AND THEN WHAT?
WE'LL TRY A COUPLE OF DIFFERENT APPROACHES, SINCE WE'RE DEALING WITH ENERGIES NO ONE'S EVER SEEN BEFORE.
SERGEANT SANDERSON IS TAKING A TRADITIONAL "HARD SCIENCE" APPROACH.
HE BELIEVES HE CAN CURE YOU BY REVERSING THE RADIATION THAT MADE YOU SHRINK. THAT'S APPROACH ALPHA.
SERGEANT FONG, ON THE OTHER HAND, BELIEVES ***YOU*** CAN REVERSE THIS PROCESS USING THE POWER OF YOUR OWN MIND, FOCUSED THROUGH THESE CRYSTALS.
WE'RE CALLING THAT APPROACH BETA.
IT'S YOUR CHOICE WHICH ONE TO TRY FIRST.

GO ON TO THE NEXT PAGE.

Hard science . . . or mind power.
But what if you just hold off for a while?

WILL YOU . . .

. . . give Sanderson's Approach Alpha a try?

TURN TO PAGE 110.

. . . go with Fong's Approach Beta?

TURN TO PAGE 109.

. . . decide you don't like either of those?

TURN TO PAGE 103.

You're not sure how to approach the colossal giant alien boy floating by himself in the park. He seems very intent on his book—if that *is* a book. You definitely don't want to startle him. You know how you'd react if a tiny, glowing person walked up and said hello to you, and it might end up with a tiny, glowing, *squished* person.

"H-hello?" you call out. The boy looks around but can't tell where your voice came from. "Down here!" You wave your arms and jump up and down.

He sees you then, and his eyes get *huge*. He looks around to see if anyone else is watching, then floats down to the ground and puts the book around you like a screen.

"Who are you?" he asks. "*What* are you? How'd you get here?"

GO ON TO THE NEXT PAGE.

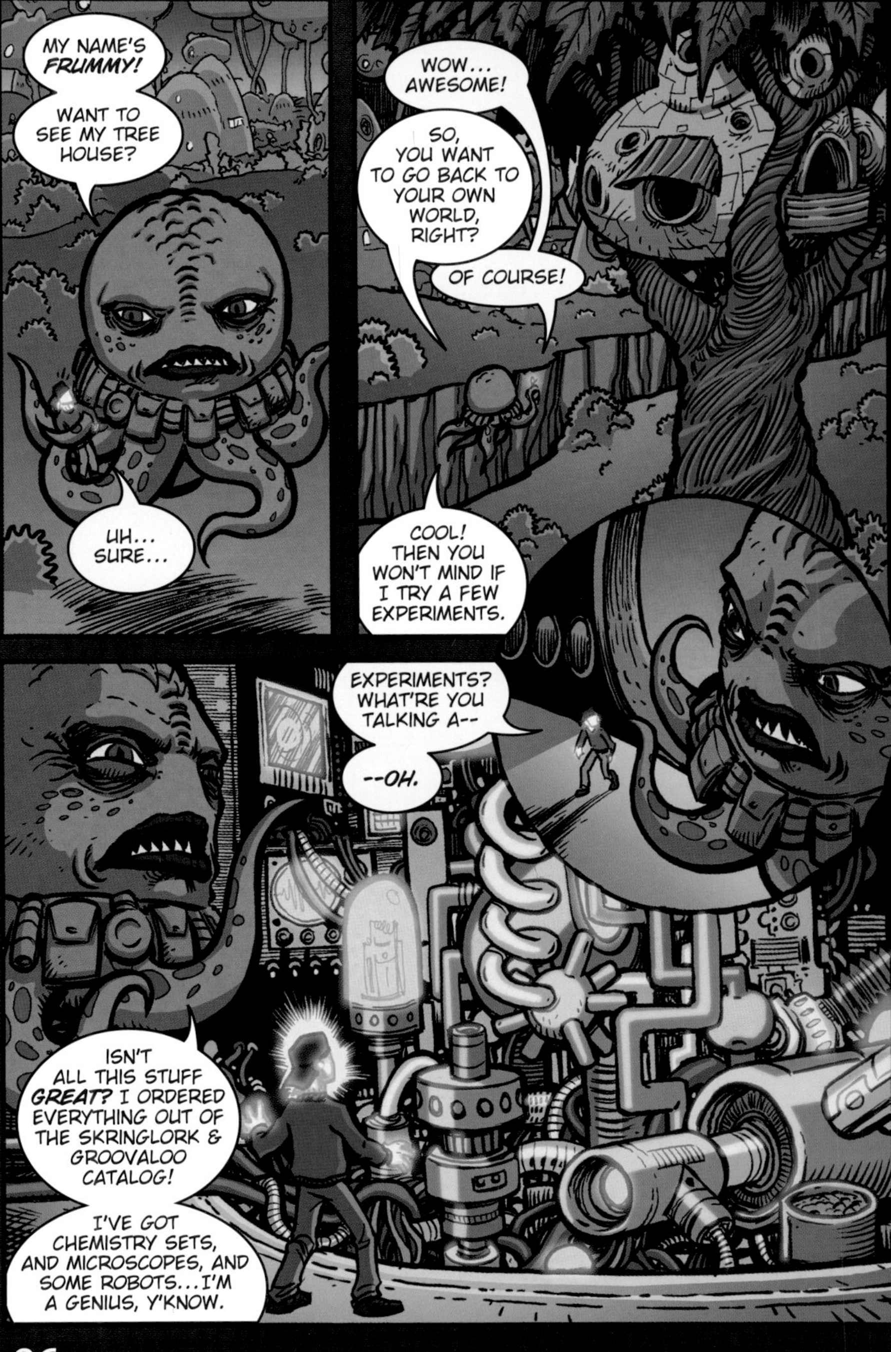

MY NAME'S *FRUMMY!*
WANT TO SEE MY TREE HOUSE?
UH... SURE...
WOW... AWESOME!
SO, YOU WANT TO GO BACK TO YOUR OWN WORLD, RIGHT?
OF COURSE!
COOL! THEN YOU WON'T MIND IF I TRY A FEW EXPERIMENTS.
EXPERIMENTS? WHAT'RE YOU TALKING A--
--OH.
ISN'T ALL THIS STUFF *GREAT?* I ORDERED EVERYTHING OUT OF THE SKRINGLORK & GROOVALOO CATALOG!
I'VE GOT CHEMISTRY SETS, AND MICROSCOPES, AND SOME ROBOTS... I'M A GENIUS, Y'KNOW.

TURN TO PAGE 65.

And then . . .

. . . everything falls silent.

No more meteors fall. The storm is over! You're left, standing on top of the city's tallest building, and you realize you've done it! You've saved the city!

Then the silence is broken by the sounds of people shouting and, even more loudly, the noise of approaching helicopters. You're about to get plastered all over every TV station in the country. Maybe *even* the world.

You're not ready for that kind of exposure. You nudge the nearby glowing yellow meteorite with one toe . . .

. . . and, just as you hoped, seconds later, you've shrunk back down to your normal size.

You slip away into the shadows and make your way downstairs, just as everyone else converges on the rooftop. Nobody will ever know who stopped the meteors . . .

. . . and that's *just fine* with you.

THE END

You agree to help and follow the commissioner's helicopter as he leads you toward the giant monster. You have to be really careful only to walk on the streets, and even then, you end up accidentally stepping on a couple of parked cars.

"Okay!" the commissioner shouts to you. "It's right around there!" He points to a cluster of tall buildings, and sure enough, you can hear a serious ruckus coming from that direction.

"I'll take care of it, sir," you tell him and head that way.

You almost gasp when you first catch sight of the creature. It looks like 50 percent spider, 50 percent lizard, and 100 percent gross. Plus, it's about as big as you are!

"Good grief," you whisper. "Where'd *you* come from?"

The monster catches sight of you and growls.

Nearby you can see the lake you threw the car into . . . and a huge bank of power lines.

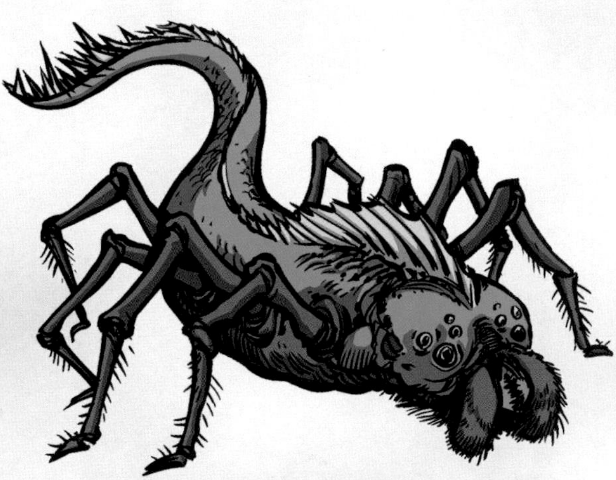

GO ON TO THE NEXT PAGE.

TWISTED JOURNEYS®

It could destroy the whole city . . .
and who knows where it would stop?

WILL YOU . . .

. . . drive the monster into the lake?
TURN TO PAGE 96.

. . . try to wrap the monster up
in the power lines?
TURN TO PAGE 41.

"Oooh, you're so smart!" Kaurie says as she takes you from Skurg. Skurg scowls and floats away. "Let's take you home!"

"Y'know," you shout, since you have to shout for her to hear you, "I'd really like to go back where I came from. Could you help me?"

"Of course I can help you!" she says. "I'll take good care of you!"

Kaurie ignores your further protests and takes you to her house, which is the size of an entire skyscraper in the normal world. She floats through a window, into her room . . . and drops you into a big glass jar! "Hey!" you scream. "Get me out of here!"

But Kaurie punches holes in the jar's metal lid and screws it on tight. Then she taps on the glass. "Do you like your new home, pixie? I'll take care of you forever and ever!"

Forever.

You're pretty sure she means it.

THE END

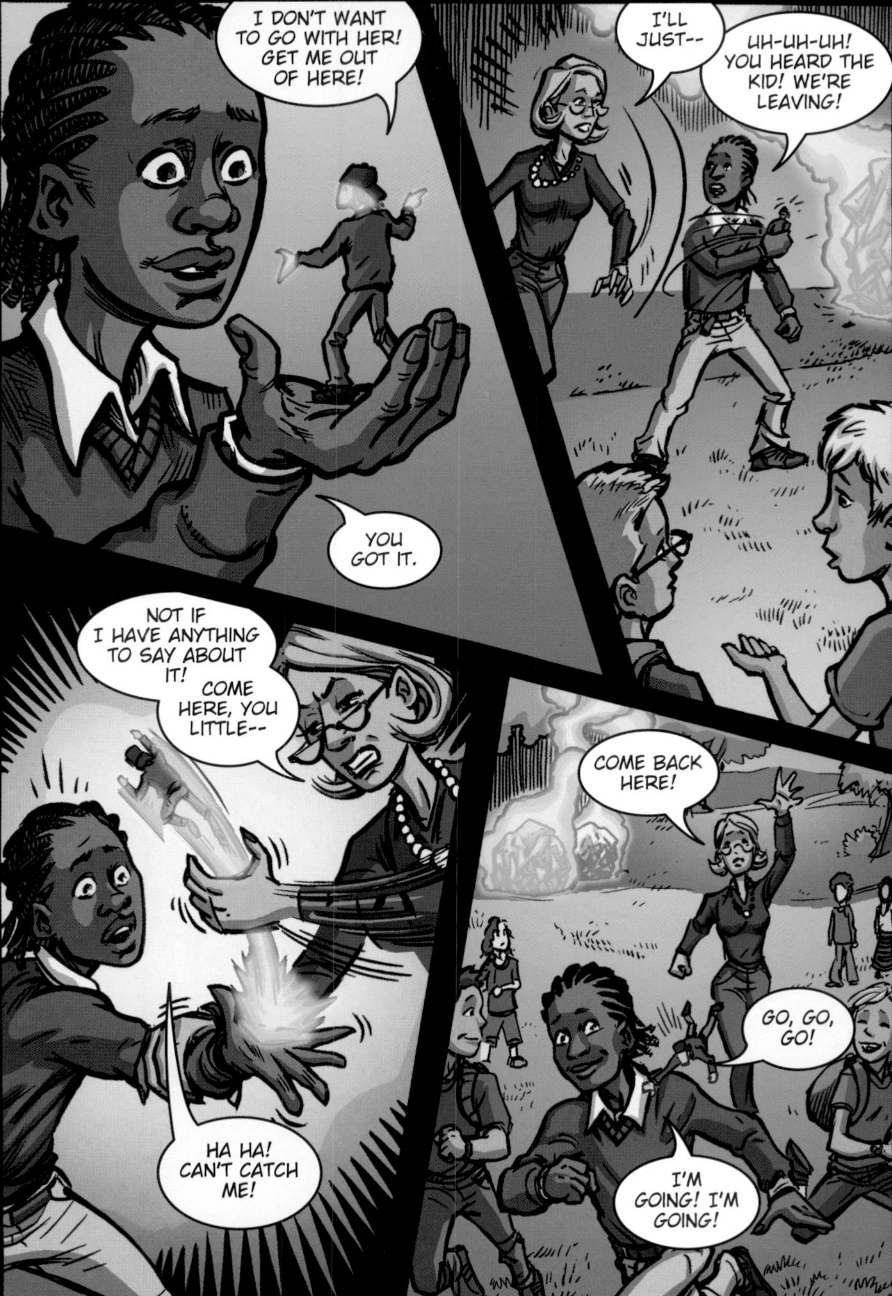

I DON'T WANT TO GO WITH HER! GET ME OUT OF HERE!
YOU GOT IT.
I'LL JUST--
UH-UH-UH! YOU HEARD THE KID! WE'RE LEAVING!
NOT IF I HAVE ANYTHING TO SAY ABOUT IT!
COME HERE, YOU LITTLE--
HA HA! CAN'T CATCH ME!
COME BACK HERE!
GO, GO, GO!
I'M GOING! I'M GOING!

As Miss Fitch shouts after you, LeBron and several of your other classmates take off running toward the edge of the park, away from the glowing crystal meteorites. You can hear more sirens as emergency services start to respond to the bizarre incident.

Finally, your friends stop running, and LeBron brings you up to eye level with him. "This is so cool!" he says. "You're so *tiny*! Awesome!"

You look down at yourself. "Yeah, it's okay, I guess," you tell him. "Not sure I want to stay this way, though."

LeBron's eyes light up. "Hey, maybe if I touch that crystal, I'll shrink too!"

"Ooh, me too!" one of your other friends says, and then more of them join in: "Me too! Me too!"

You can still see the glowing crystal, out in the middle of the park. You're not convinced touching that crystal is a good idea.

GO ON TO THE NEXT PAGE.

You know what the weird meteorite did to *you* . . . but who knows what it might do to *them*?

WILL YOU . . .

. . . tell your friends that being this tiny is no fun at all?
TURN TO PAGE 50.

. . . agree that it might be fun if you were all the same size?
TURN TO PAGE 87.

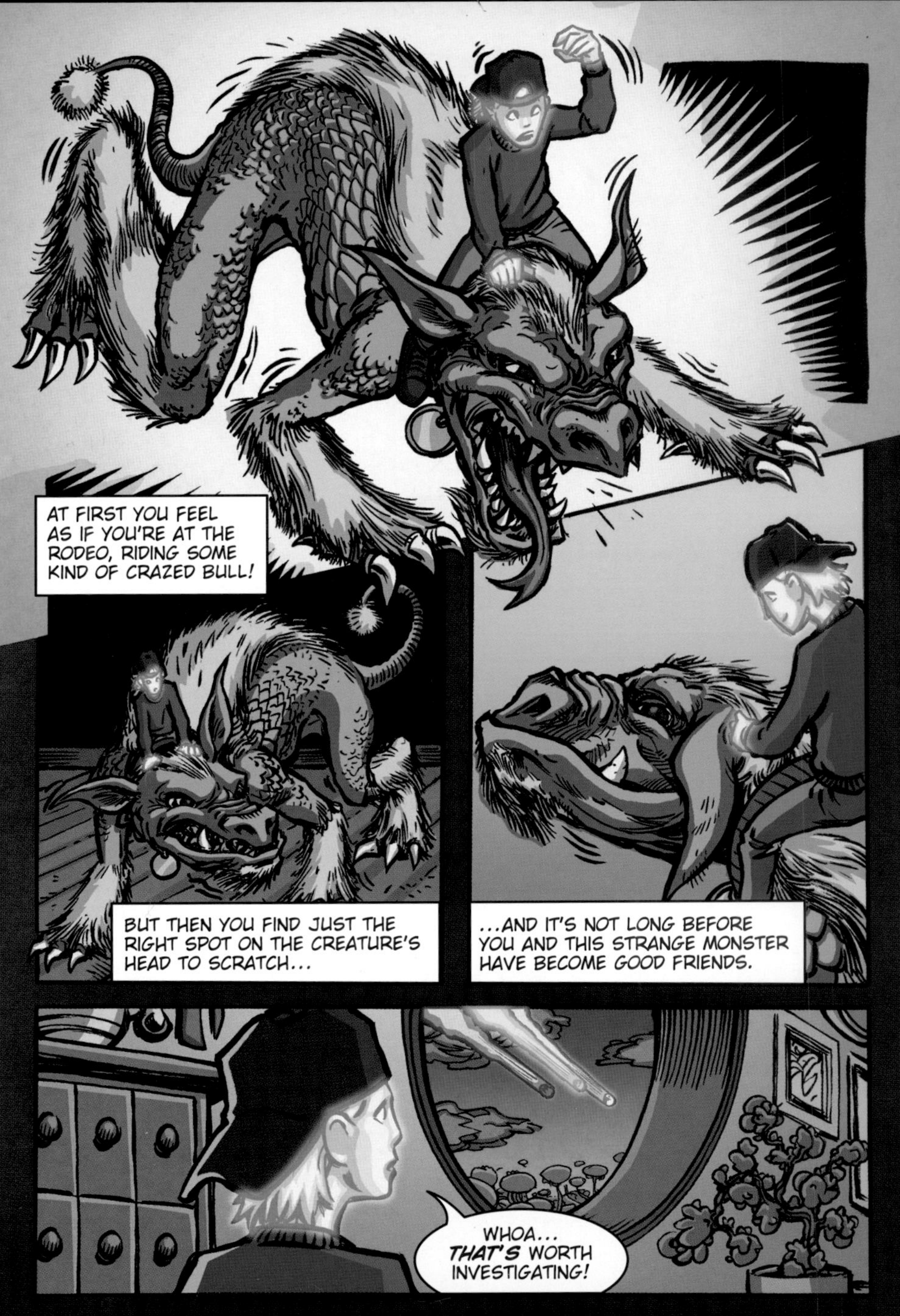

AT FIRST YOU FEEL AS IF YOU'RE AT THE RODEO, RIDING SOME KIND OF CRAZED BULL!
BUT THEN YOU FIND JUST THE RIGHT SPOT ON THE CREATURE'S HEAD TO SCRATCH...
...AND IT'S NOT LONG BEFORE YOU AND THIS STRANGE MONSTER HAVE BECOME GOOD FRIENDS.
WHOA... ***THAT'S*** WORTH INVESTIGATING!

GO ON TO THE NEXT PAGE.

Perched on the pet's head, you lean down and speak into its ear. "I need to go look at those meteors outside," you tell it. "Can you help me?"

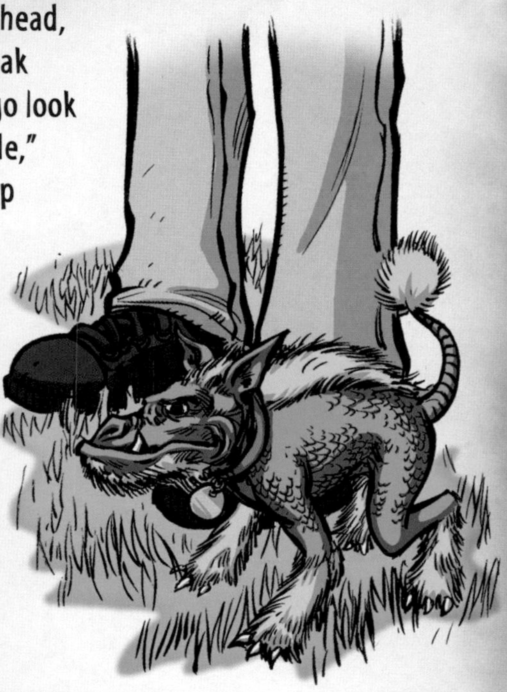

The pet turns and, with your guidance, jumps out an open window. "Over there! Good doggie! Good doggie!"

You can see a familiar yellow glow as you and the scaly creature approach the crash site. The pet takes you straight to the meteor. You reach out and touch it . . .

There's an explosion of golden light—

—and suddenly you're back in the park, standing next to LeBron!

"Hey, where you been?" he asks. Then he looks down at your feet. "And—*aaaah! What is that thing?!*"

You bend down and pick up the creature, which now fits comfortably in the crook of your arm. It licks you happily. "Something for show-and-tell," you say, smiling.

THE END

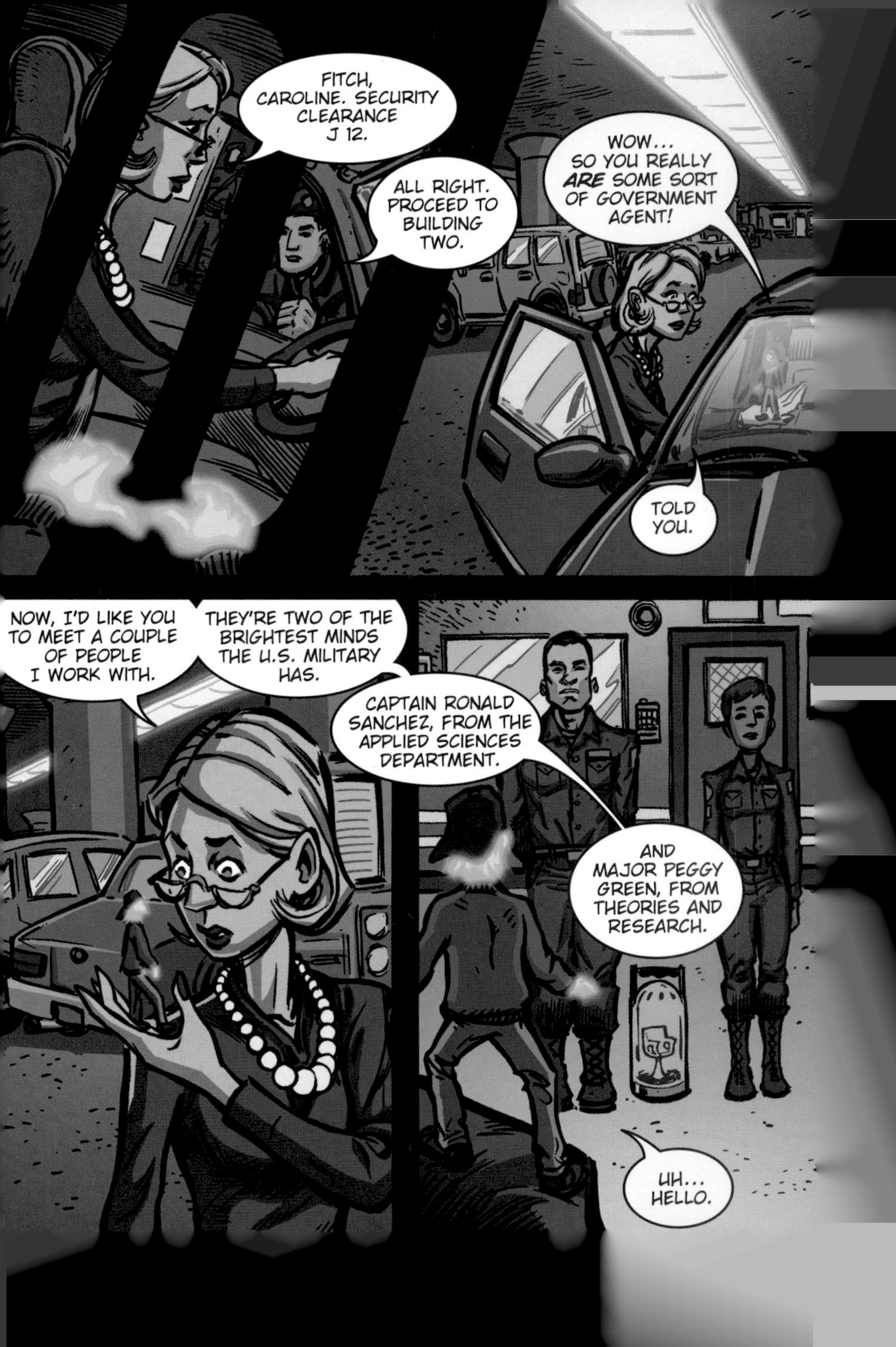
FITCH, CAROLINE. SECURITY CLEARANCE J 12.
ALL RIGHT. PROCEED TO BUILDING TWO.
WOW... SO YOU REALLY *ARE* SOME SORT OF GOVERNMENT AGENT!
TOLD YOU.
NOW, I'D LIKE YOU TO MEET A COUPLE OF PEOPLE I WORK WITH.
THEY'RE TWO OF THE BRIGHTEST MINDS THE U.S. MILITARY HAS.
CAPTAIN RONALD SANCHEZ, FROM THE APPLIED SCIENCES DEPARTMENT.
AND MAJOR PEGGY GREEN, FROM THEORIES AND RESEARCH.
UH... HELLO.

"They're looking at me funny," you whisper in Miss Fitch's ear.

"Don't worry," she says, smiling. "Whatever it is that's happened to you, one of them can figure it out."

Sanchez and Green both say hello, but they're still giving you the eyeball as if you're some sort of precious gem. "Amazing," Sanchez says softly. "And it happened in seconds? The size modification? *Amazing*."

"Don't treat the child like a scientific curiosity, Ron," Major Green says. "We have to look at the potential involved here."

Miss Fitch tells you, "These are the two brightest scientific minds the military has to offer. If anybody can figure out what's going on with you, one of them can." She paused. "But you have to decide which, because they work in two completely different departments, and they can't both help you."

You look from Green to Sanchez and back again.

GO ON TO THE NEXT PAGE.

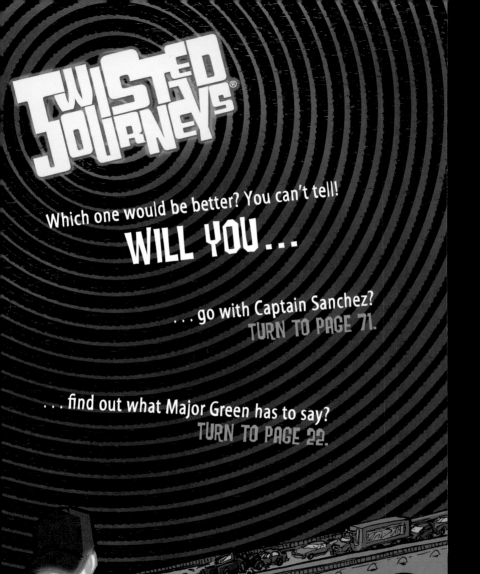

Which one would be better? You can't tell!

WILL YOU...

...go with Captain Sanchez?
TURN TO PAGE 71.

...find out what Major Green has to say?
TURN TO PAGE 22.

Your new giant legs are so long, it only takes a few steps to get you far away from all the clustering police. You hop over a river and crouch down among some tall trees. From there you can see the sky clearly.

It's like watching a sparkling, yellow and green rain shower. Meteors streak across the sky, more and more of them . . . and it looks as if they're headed straight for the closest city.

A few of them start to hit the ground near you, and despite your size, the impacts jar you. Standing up again, you look around. There's a big freeway overpass nearby and a big construction site up on a hill. Plus, it wouldn't take long to get over the city if you decided to run.

The impacts get worse and worse all around you. You see meteors smash into the city's buildings.

TURN TO PAGE 61.

TWISTED JOURNEYS®

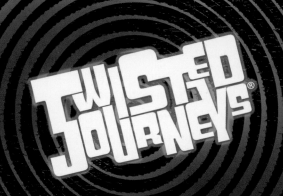

With that robot thing behind you, you've got to make a decision, *right now*!

WILL YOU . . .

. . . rush through the door made of cardboard?
TURN TO PAGE 45.

. . . try the metal door instead?
TURN TO PAGE 8.

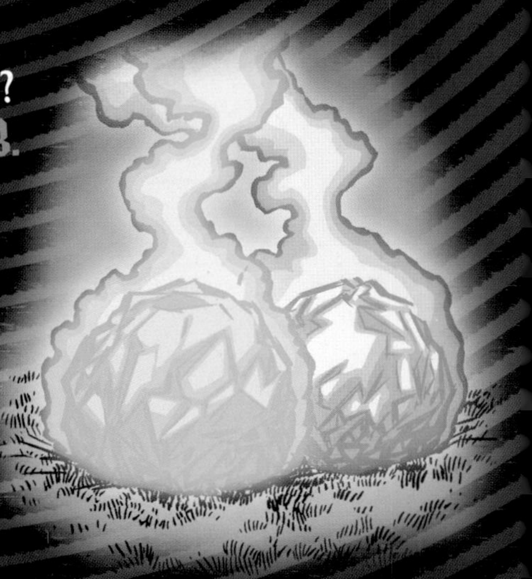

You've seen enough monster movies to know what happens when a gigantic mutant or alien or something blunders into a bunch of power lines. Snap, sizzle, pop!

"Here, lizard, lizard, lizard," you call out, beckoning to it with your hands. "Come on, that's a good giant bug thing!"

The spider-lizard blinks eight of its eyes at you, snarls, and charges! You barely get out of the way as it rushes past you. But you're not at the power lines yet. "Missed me, ugly face!" you shout as you edge into position. One more rush and it'll run right into the lines. The creature gets ready to charge again . . .

. . . but instead, it fires a huge glob of *web* at you! The putrid, sticky gunk binds itself to you and wraps your arms tight around your body. One more blob and your legs are bound . . .

. . . and you topple directly into the power lines.

Snap.

Sizzle.

Pop.

Just like in the monster movies.

THE END

41

You've shrunk down to the size of one of the insects you were just trying to catch! How? Why?

You don't have time to think about these things, because one of your classmates takes a step toward you, and the shock wave of his foot coming down almost knocks you over. One of your friends could squash you flat without even realizing it! You've got to get away from here!

The blades of grass look as tall as trees to you as you sprint away from all the other kids—kids who tower over you like something out of a monster movie. Their voices sound distorted, as if they're *roaring*, and it hurts your tiny ears.

The ground starts to rise, and you sprint out of the grass and onto a vast, perfectly flat white plain. It takes you a second to realize you're on a concrete bike path!

GO ON TO THE NEXT PAGE.

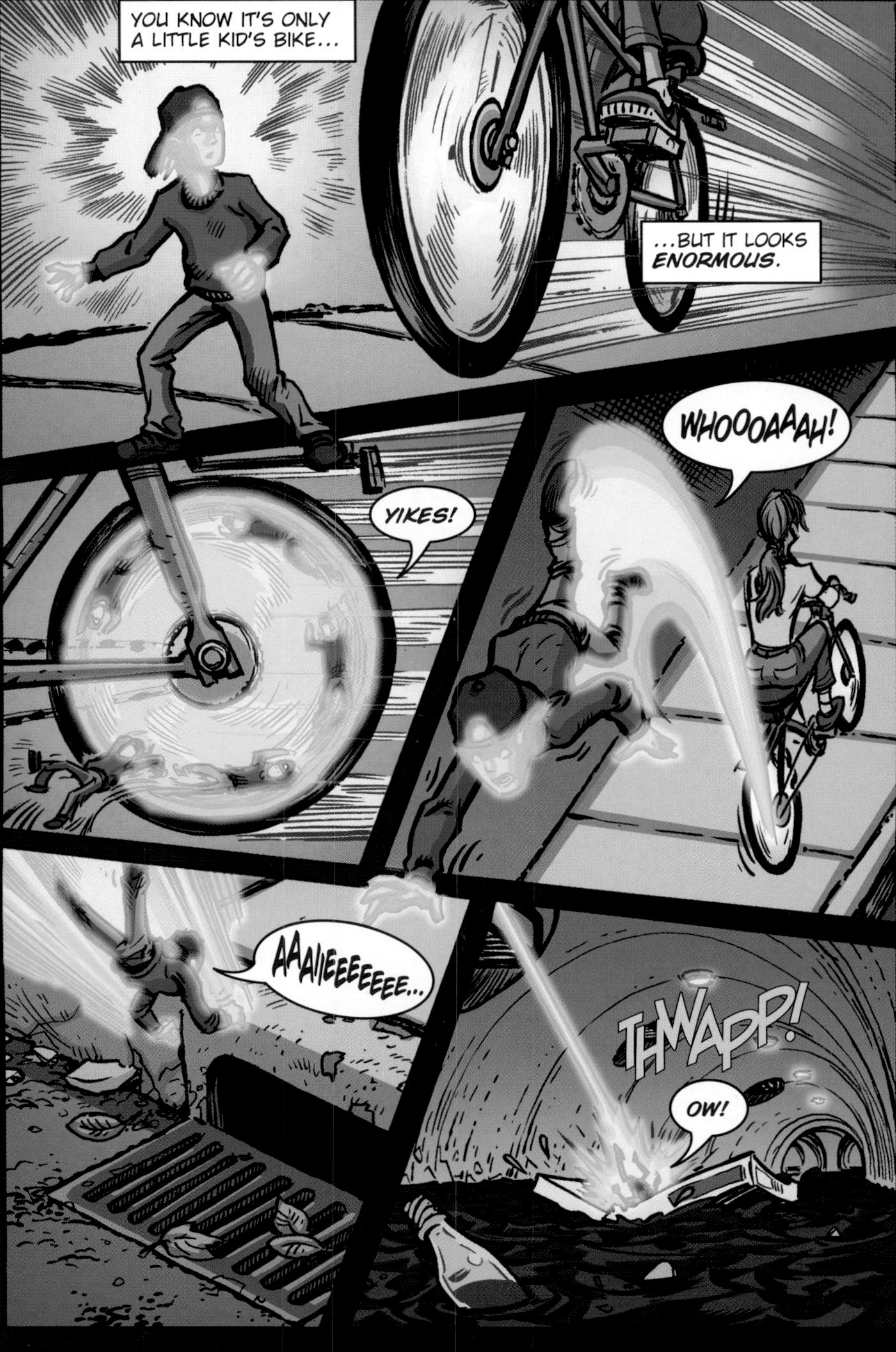
YOU KNOW IT'S ONLY A LITTLE KID'S BIKE...
...BUT IT LOOKS ENORMOUS.
YIKES!
WHOOOAAAH!
AAAIIEEEEEEE...
THWAPP!
OW!

As small as you are, this place looks more like an alien planet than a sewer.

WILL YOU...

...jump off and swim for the side with the concrete curb?
TURN TO PAGE 54.

...stay on the box and see where the water takes you?
TURN TO PAGE 70.

...try to make it over to the side with the sandy shore?
TURN TO PAGE 89.

The cardboard door swings open. You stumble out of the maze and onto the tree house floor, immensely relieved that the robot creature isn't following you. But that relief doesn't last long, as suddenly a cage drops down from above and traps you!

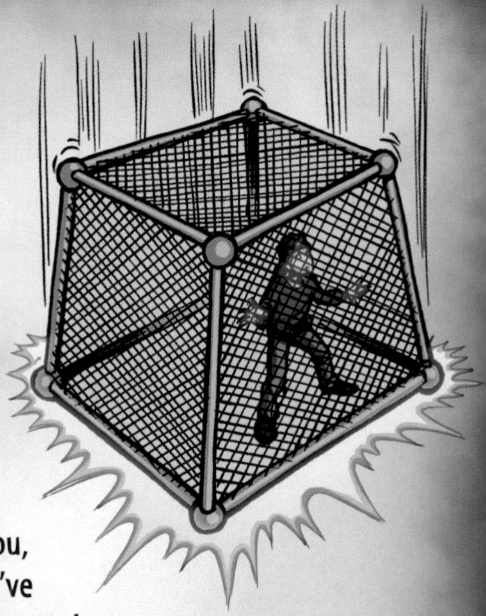

Frummy floats toward you, tentacles waving. "I think I've got it figured out!" he says—and you see that he's setting up the colossal machine so that it's pointing right at you. "If the math is right, this Wave Inducer will send you straight home. It's gonna be *so cool!*"

"Wait!" you scream, but he hits the switch anyway. There's a blinding flash of purple light . . .

. . . and abruptly you find yourself in the park, looking at Miss Fitch and the rest of your classmates.

"Where have you *been*?" she demands frantically. "What happened?"

You sigh. "You might call it a tall tale," you say and chuckle to yourself.

THE END

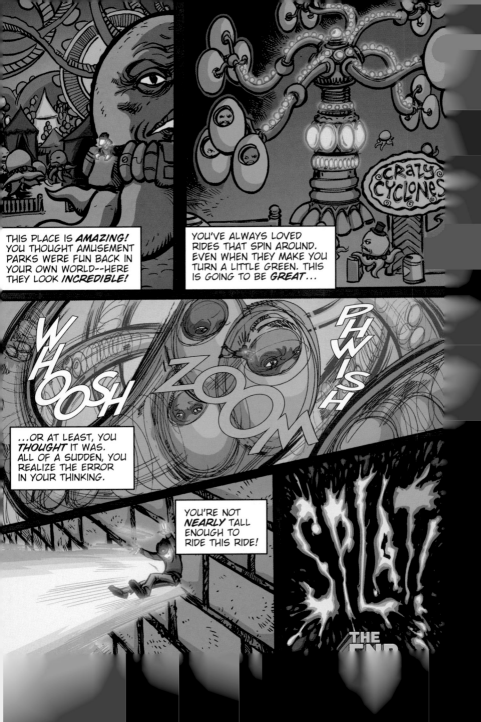

THIS PLACE IS *AMAZING!* YOU THOUGHT AMUSEMENT PARKS WERE FUN BACK IN YOUR OWN WORLD--HERE THEY LOOK *INCREDIBLE!*

YOU'VE ALWAYS LOVED RIDES THAT SPIN AROUND. EVEN WHEN THEY MAKE YOU TURN A LITTLE GREEN. THIS IS GOING TO BE *GREAT...*

CRAZY CYCLONES

WHOOSH

ZOOM

PHWISH

...OR AT LEAST, YOU *THOUGHT* IT WAS. ALL OF A SUDDEN, YOU REALIZE THE ERROR IN YOUR THINKING.

YOU'RE NOT *NEARLY* TALL ENOUGH TO RIDE THIS RIDE!

SPLAT!

THE END

You can't take all the shrinking and growing and shrinking and growing! Much more of this will tear you apart! Without really thinking about it, you reach out one gigantic hand and grab the meteorite . . .

. . . and, to your astonishment, when you shrink again, *it shrinks with you.*

Not only that, but the shrinking feels slower. More controlled. And when you reach your normal size and appearance, you look down at the red and purple rock in your hand. And you *think* about getting bigger.

Suddenly you start growing again! *Stop*, you say to yourself—and you *do* stop.

"I can control it!" you shout out loud. Concentrating on the stone again, you grow back up to your full giant height. You laugh and whisper, "Here comes the giant!"

Then you shrink back down again, becoming an average, everyday kid.

You drop the stone in your pocket.

That'll come in handy.

TURN TO PAGE 69.

There's *way* too much chance of getting squished if you stay in that lunch box. You crawl out and take a look around. One of the alien kids is wearing a beltlike harness, and a big floppy bag hangs off it. Maybe . . . if you're quick . . .

It only takes a second to climb onto the bag and crawl in. You can even peek out from a tiny hole in the fabric and sort of see where you're going . . .

. . . and you get a good look at a huge floating sign as the blimp passes it. . . . It looks like an ad for some kind of gigantic alien amusement park.

The owner of the bag you're hiding in says, "I can't wait to see the science exhibit."

The boy next to her says, "BO-ring. I'm headed straight for the Crazy Cyclones!"

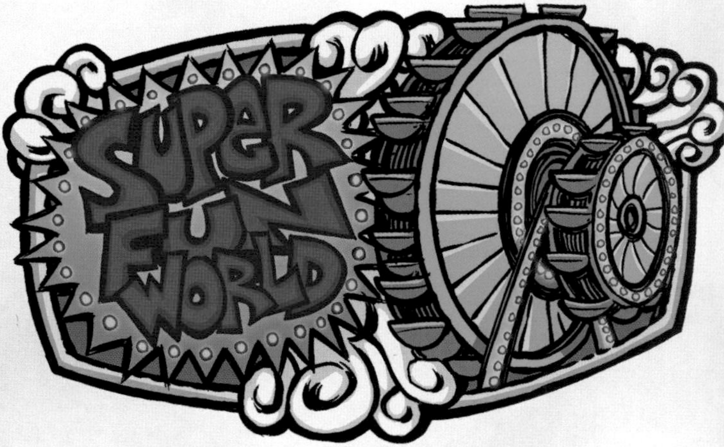
SUPER FUN WORLD

GO ON TO THE NEXT PAGE.

Science exhibit? Crazy Cyclones? You don't know what to expect from either one of those things.

WILL YOU...

...tag along with the girl as she goes to the science exhibit hall?
TURN TO PAGE 80.

...jump into the bag of the boy going to the Crazy Cyclones?
TURN TO PAGE 46.

"Trust me, being this size kind of stinks," you tell LeBron. "Besides, for all we know, touching that thing might turn you into a chicken or make you a hundred feet tall! Let's forget about the crystals. I just want to go home, where it's safe."

"Oh . . . okay." LeBron seems disappointed, but he's not arguing with you. "I'll get you home. Let me just tell Miss Fitch where we're going."

LeBron carries you over to Miss Fitch and tells her he's taking you back to your house.

"No!" she cries. "Nobody can leave till this whole thing is investigated! It's not safe!" Miss Fitch tries to grab LeBron, but the other kids stand in the way.

Then LeBron loses his grip on you. You tumble out of his hand and land on the crystal, which glows and hums.

Instantly, you start to grow again! In seconds, you're back to normal . . .

. . . and after that one last burst of energy, the crystals both disintegrate into dust right before your eyes.

You're sure of one thing: you're never going to feel short again.

THE END

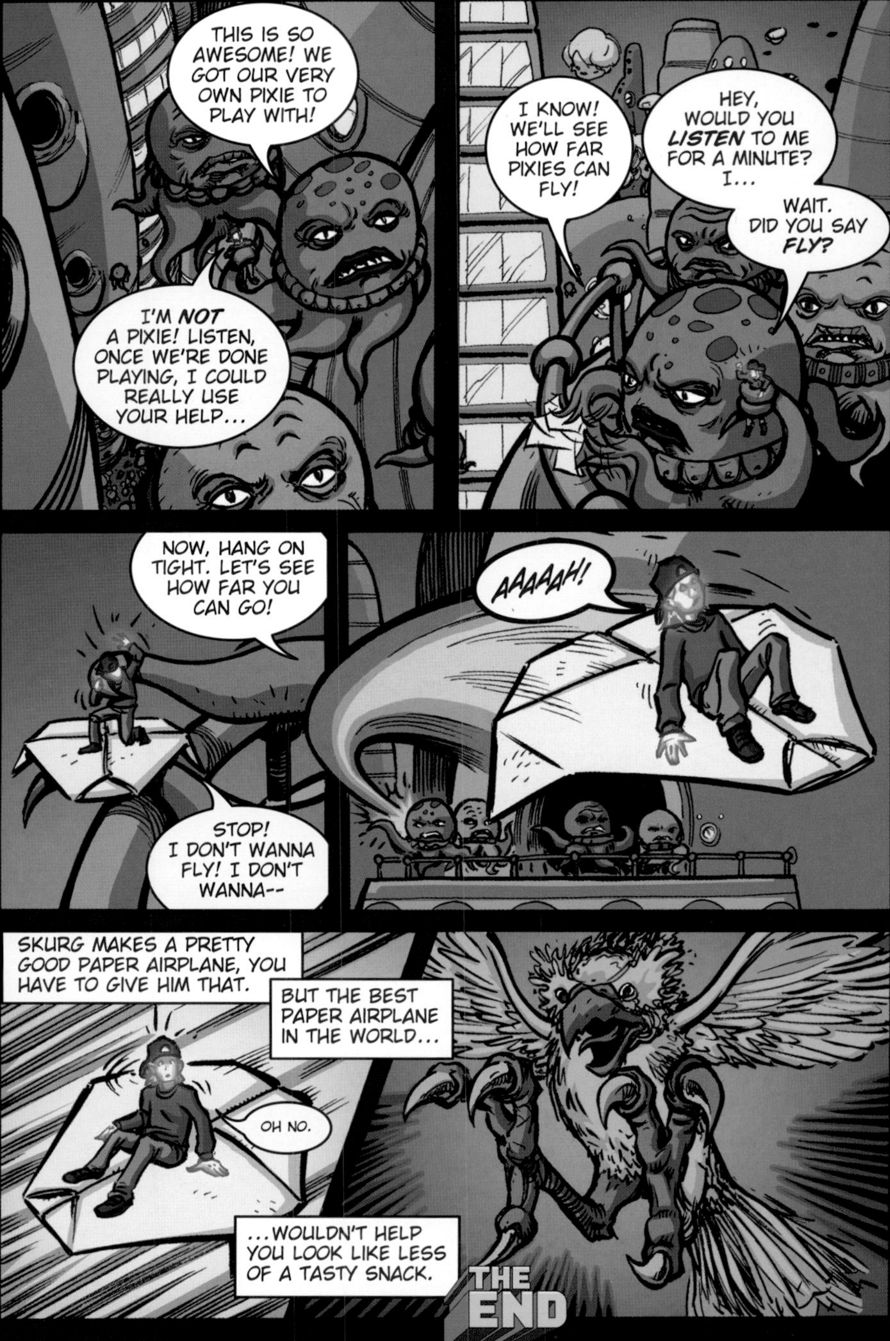
THIS IS SO AWESOME! WE GOT OUR VERY OWN PIXIE TO PLAY WITH!
I'M NOT A PIXIE! LISTEN, ONCE WE'RE DONE PLAYING, I COULD REALLY USE YOUR HELP...
I KNOW! WE'LL SEE HOW FAR PIXIES CAN FLY!
HEY, WOULD YOU LISTEN TO ME FOR A MINUTE? I...
WAIT. DID YOU SAY FLY?
NOW, HANG ON TIGHT. LET'S SEE HOW FAR YOU CAN GO!
STOP! I DON'T WANNA FLY! I DON'T WANNA--
AAAAAH!
SKURG MAKES A PRETTY GOOD PAPER AIRPLANE, YOU HAVE TO GIVE HIM THAT.
BUT THE BEST PAPER AIRPLANE IN THE WORLD...
OH NO.
...WOULDN'T HELP YOU LOOK LIKE LESS OF A TASTY SNACK.
THE END

The tests go on for so long you start to get tired. "I think I'd better call my parents now," you tell Captain Sanchez.

"We're making the necessary arrangements," he tells you. "Here, why don't you lie down for a while first?" Sanchez puts you down next to the hamster-house setup on the table. It has a perfect little bedroom, and you can't deny that the bed looks awfully comfortable.

"Okay," you say. "I guess I could rest my eyes awhile." It doesn't take long for you to fall asleep.

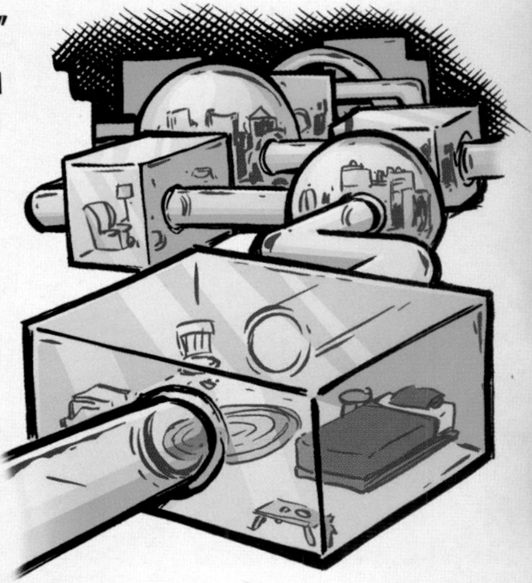

When you wake up, Sanchez is there, watching you. *Creepy!* "I'm ready for that phone call now," you tell him.

"Oh, there won't be any phone calls." Sanchez grins a humorless grin. "We've decided that you'll be staying here. Doing tests. *From now on.*"

A lab rat . . . ?

Not what you were planning to be for the rest of your life!

THE END

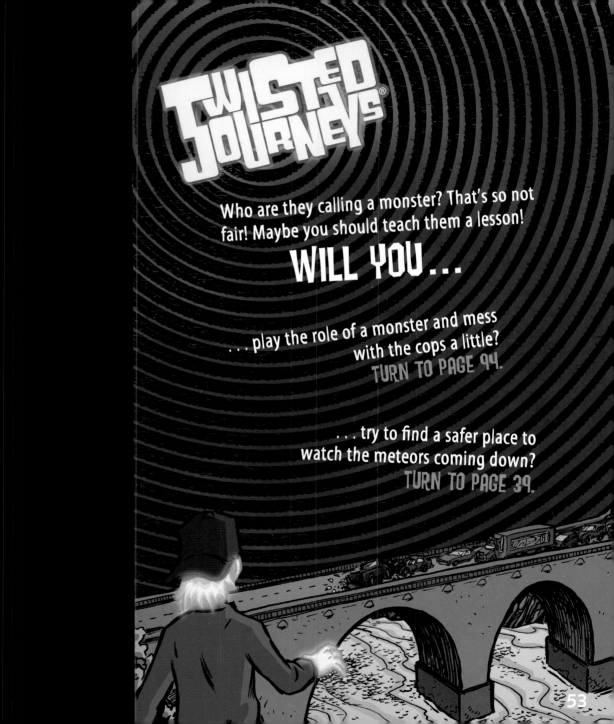

Who are they calling a monster? That's so not fair! Maybe you should teach them a lesson!

WILL YOU...

. . . play the role of a monster and mess with the cops a little?
TURN TO PAGE 94.

. . . try to find a safer place to watch the meteors coming down?
TURN TO PAGE 39.

You hold your breath and jump off, kicking and stroking until you get to the side. Some moss grows on the concrete there, and you climb up until you reach a dry ledge.

Far above you, you can see a spot of sunlight! You realize you're looking at a gap in a manhole cover. If you can get up there, you can get out of the sewer.

The same moss grows up the side of the tunnel, and you start climbing again. It's not too hard, especially now that you weigh practically nothing. You hear a strange rumbling sound from up above, but you don't let that stop you. You climb higher and higher . . . and the sound gets louder and louder . . .

. . . and just as you reach the surface, something like a tornado yanks you off your feet! The noise was a street sweeper . . . and you're about to get cleaned up for good. . . !

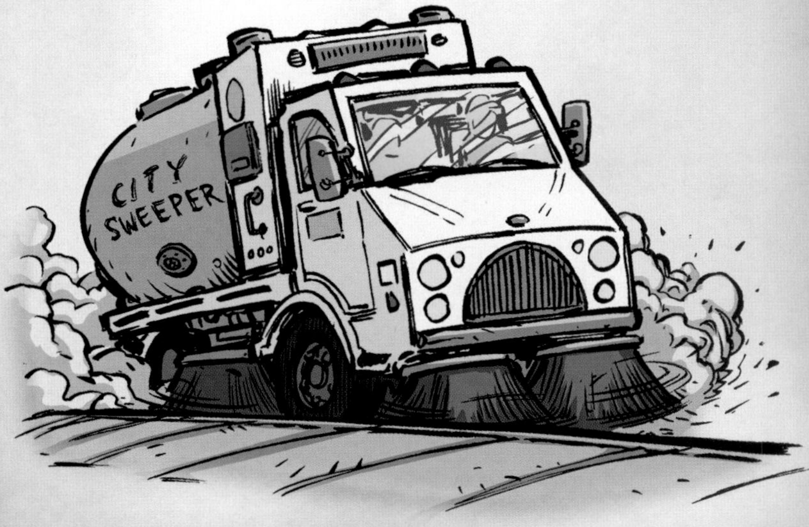
CITY
SWEEPER

THE END

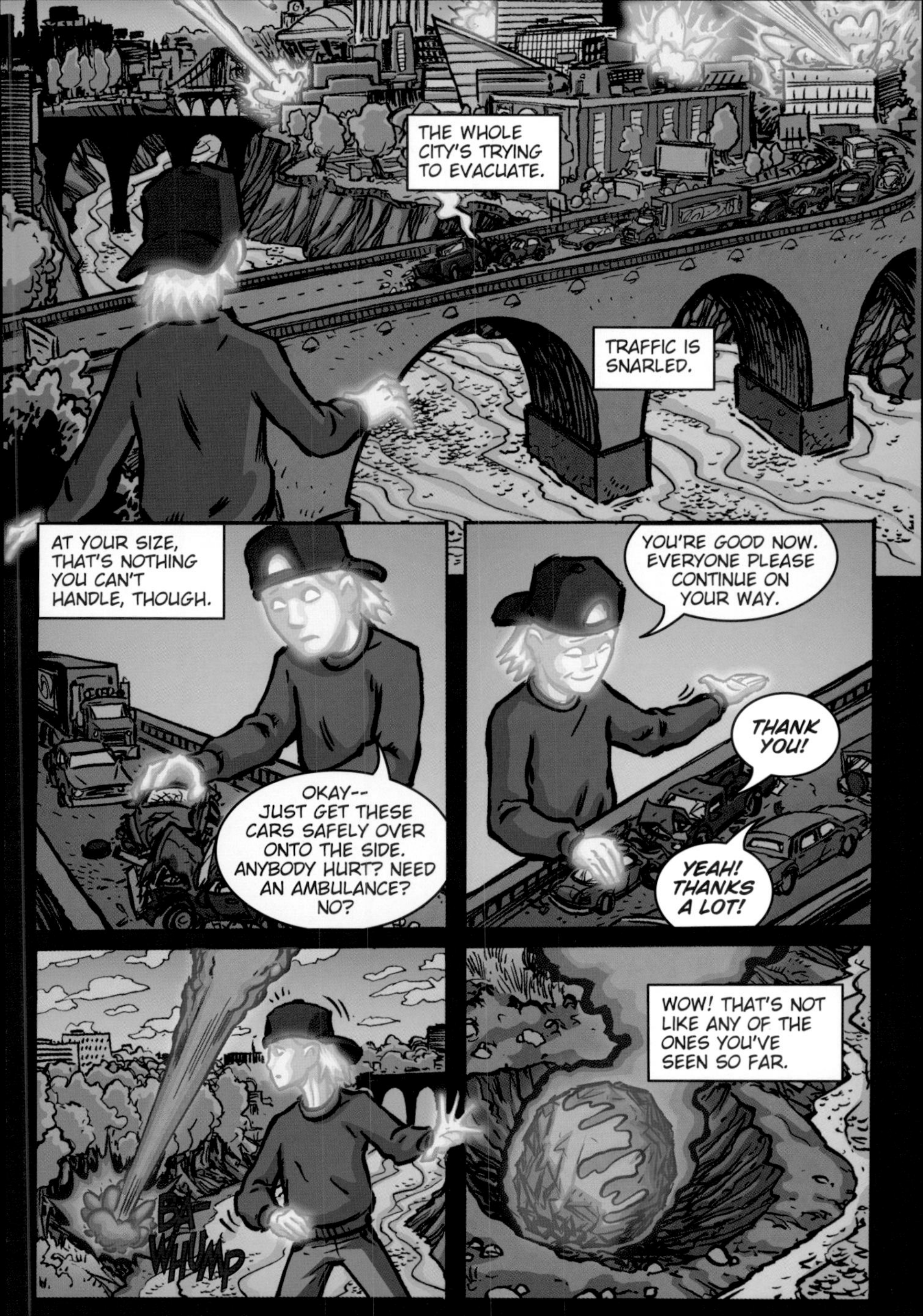
THE WHOLE CITY'S TRYING TO EVACUATE.
TRAFFIC IS SNARLED.
AT YOUR SIZE, THAT'S NOTHING YOU CAN'T HANDLE, THOUGH.
OKAY-- JUST GET THESE CARS SAFELY OVER ONTO THE SIDE. ANYBODY HURT? NEED AN AMBULANCE? NO?
YOU'RE GOOD NOW. EVERYONE PLEASE CONTINUE ON YOUR WAY.
THANK YOU!
YEAH! THANKS A LOT!
BA-WHUMP
WOW! THAT'S NOT LIKE ANY OF THE ONES YOU'VE SEEN SO FAR.

GO ON TO THE NEXT PAGE.

You can't help wondering what would happen if you touched this new crystal.

WILL YOU...

...touch the red part of the crystal?
TURN TO PAGE 58.

...decide not to touch it at all?
TURN TO PAGE 111.

...reach for the purple part of the meteorite?
TURN TO PAGE 90.

Your bravery and willingness to sacrifice is not lost on anyone. News of what you've done sweeps the nation and then the world. People from everywhere come to see you, and soon you get set up in a custom-built, giant-sized house in what used to be an airplane hangar.

A few days after you move into your new home, some television executives come to visit you. "We've got a deal we'd like you to consider," one of them says. "Picture this: you get your own reality TV show. A camera crew follows you around as you travel the world, helping people! You could help rebuild cities and towns after natural disasters . . . you could rescue people trapped in dangerous situations . . . and check out the title! It'd be called *The World's Biggest Hero!*

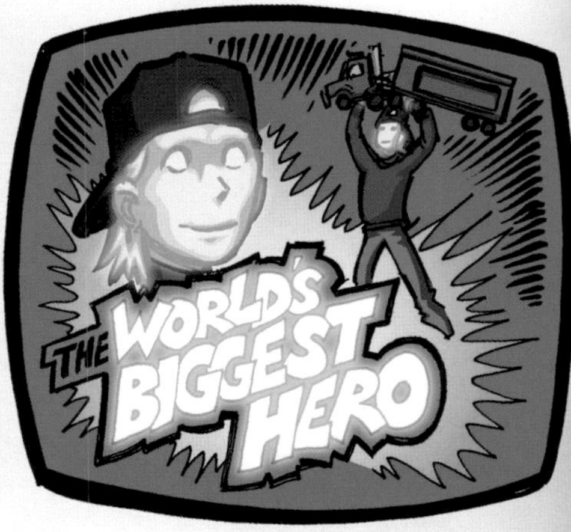
THE WORLD'S BIGGEST HERO

Travel the world? Help people? . . . Fame and fortune?

You grin down at them. "Sign me up!"

THE END

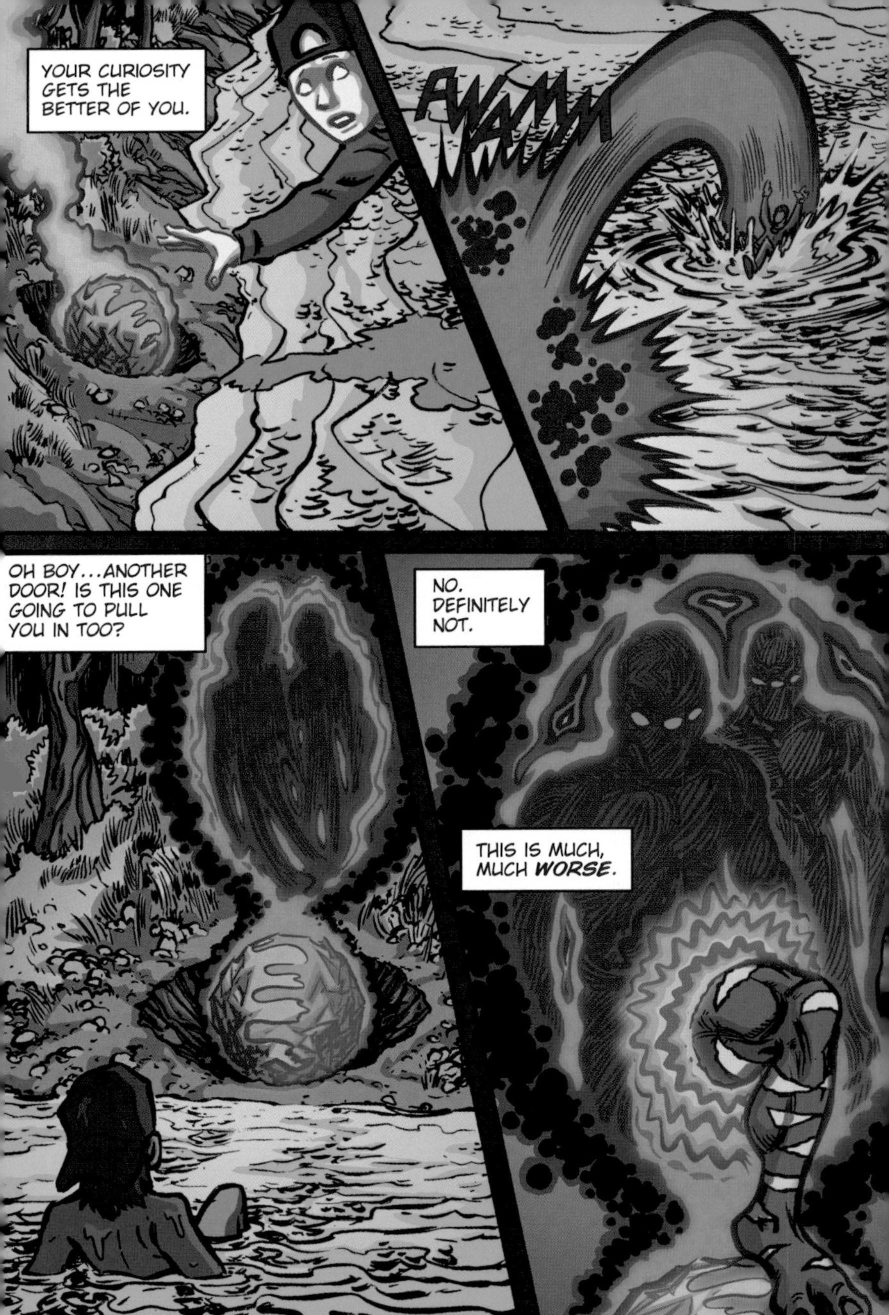
YOUR CURIOSITY GETS THE BETTER OF YOU.
FWAMM
OH BOY...ANOTHER DOOR! IS THIS ONE GOING TO PULL YOU IN TOO?
NO. DEFINITELY NOT.
THIS IS MUCH, MUCH WORSE.

The shapes get closer and closer—and then one of them steps through the doorway. You backpedal, surprised, as you realize two things. First, these creatures are giants, every bit as big as you are. Second . . . they're *terrifying*. Each one is covered in a thick purple hide with baby food yellow stripes all over it, and they have three enormous blue eyes in a row across their foreheads.

And there are a *lot* of these people. Another steps through after the first one . . . and another . . . and another. They're not stopping!

The first one glares at you. "Do you speak for this world?" he demands.

You're not sure what to say. "Uh . . . yes?"

"Then tell your people!" he bellows. "The Sarfongians have arrived to conquer your planet!"

Conquer?!

"Wait a second!" you exclaim. "Can't we talk about this?"

All his eyes narrow. "What's to talk about?"

TURN TO PAGE 82.

You have no idea what might happen, wandering around a weird alien blimp full of weird alien kids. For now, at least, you'd better just stay in the box and see where you end up.

Then suddenly the whole box is wrenched up off the floor again! "Hey! Put that down!" you hear a girl's voice say.

"If Spargle gets to grab some food, so do I!" says the boy holding the box. "Quit it! Quit trying to grab it!"

"Well put it down!" the girl shouts. "All our lunches are in there!"

"Leave me alone, or I'm throwing the whole thing out the window! Hey—I mean it—*I mean it!* Okay, you asked for it!"

You hear the sound of one of the blimp's windows opening. Wind roars into the cabin . . . and before you can do anything about it, you and the box of food are falling . . . and falling . . . and falling . . . .

THE END

Those meteors are a serious threat—but
they're just as much a threat to *you*
as to everything around you.

WILL YOU...

. . . take shelter under the overpass
and hope the meteor storm stops?
TURN TO PAGE 78.

. . . head to that construction site on higher
ground to get a better look at the area?
TURN TO PAGE 85.

. . . head straight to the city and try to help?
TURN TO PAGE 55.

"Sure, I'll help you," you tell the commissioner. "But first, I'd like to take a look at that crystal you've got there in the chopper."

The commissioner gestures, and the pilot lands the helicopter. You get down on your belly to peer into it. "Wow. That's exactly like the one I touched that got me into this whole mess."

"Could you, uh, please hurry?" the commissioner asks. "I've got reports that the monster is headed this way!"

"No problem," you tell him. "I just wanted to, y'know, poke at it." You touch it with one finger . . .

. . . and with a tremendous *BOOM*, your giant glowing body disappears, replaced with your normal-size, normal-kid one. But before you can celebrate, the ground begins to shake . . .

. . . and the other monster—a huge spider-lizard creature—comes charging straight toward you.

. . . and steps on your tiny little body with its gigantic clawed foot.

THE END

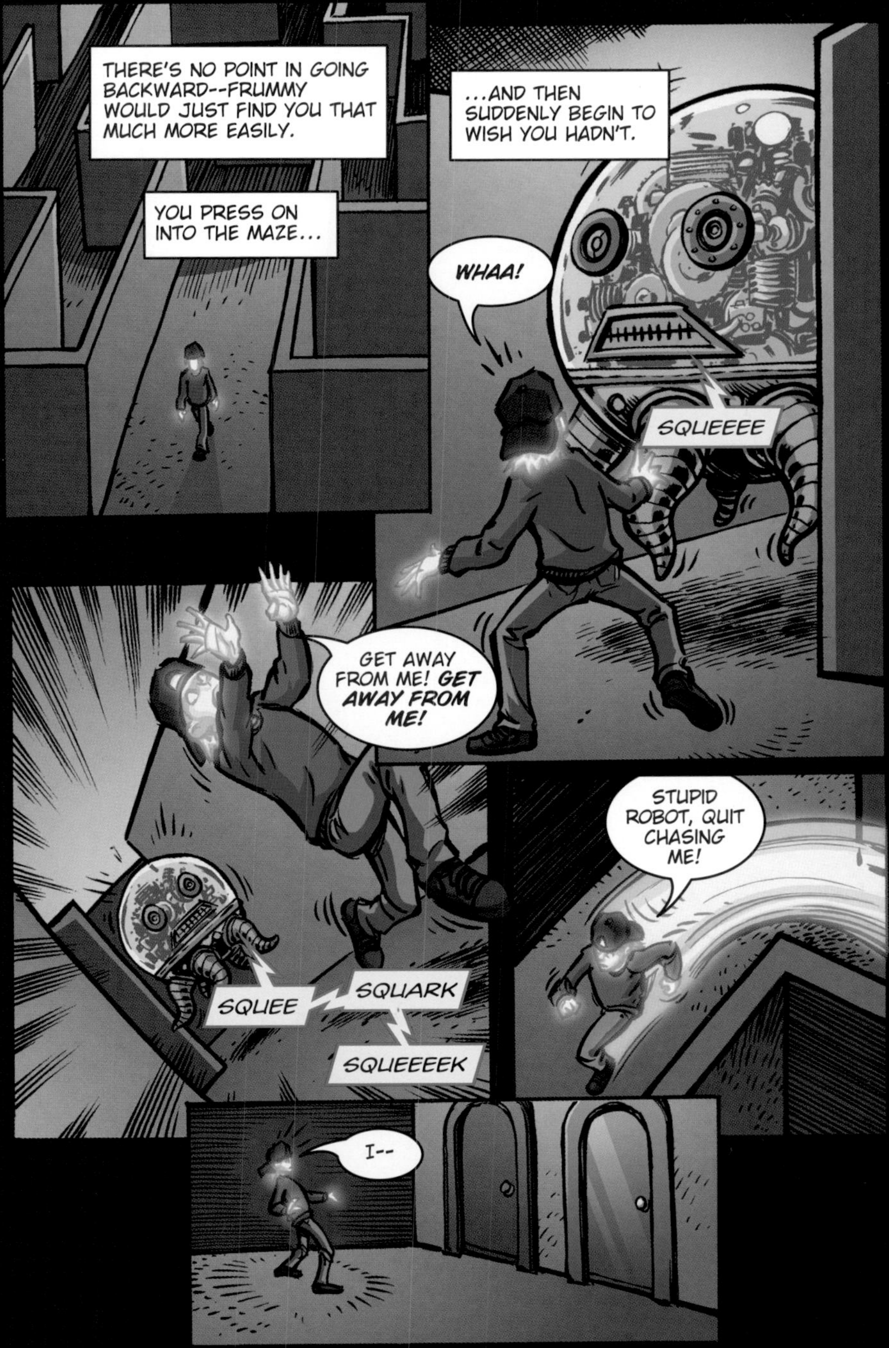
THERE'S NO POINT IN GOING BACKWARD--FRUMMY WOULD JUST FIND YOU THAT MUCH MORE EASILY.
YOU PRESS ON INTO THE MAZE...
...AND THEN SUDDENLY BEGIN TO WISH YOU HADN'T.
WHAA!
SQUEEEE
GET AWAY FROM ME! GET AWAY FROM ME!
SQUEE
SQUARK
SQUEEEEK
STUPID ROBOT, QUIT CHASING ME!
I--

TURN TO PAGE 40.

"You can forget it!" you bellow at the commissioner. "I'm having the absolute worst day of my life! Look what happened to me—a giant alien *nerd* turned me into *this*! Now you want me to fight some *monster*? I don't think so!"

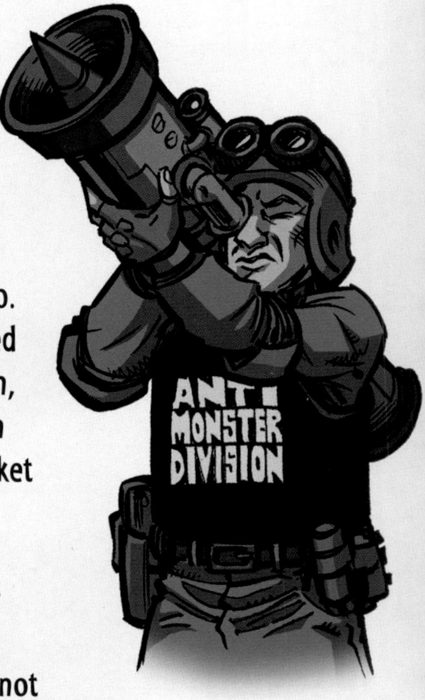
ANTI
MONSTER
DIVISION

As you've been talking, a lot more police have shown up, and now some National Guard troops are arriving too. And now that you've stopped for a second to pay attention, you notice that a lot of them have shoulder-mounted rocket launchers . . .

"Get ready to fire on the creature!" the commissioner shouts to his troops.

"Hey, wait!" you say. "I'm not saying I *won't* help. It's just that I'd prefer not to, if I could avoid it . . ."

But he's not listening. Since you refused to help, they seem to have decided you're one more giant, scary monster.

And the last thing you hear is the commissioner's voice: *"Open fire!"*

THE END

Maybe he *is* a genius. He's an alien, after all.
But he's also just a kid!

WILL YOU...

... try to hide somewhere in all the
science junk until you can get away?
TURN TO PAGE 72.

... run outside and see if a grown-up
alien can help you?
TURN TO PAGE 16.

... see if he really is a genius and let him
try to send you back home?
TURN TO PAGE 11.

A few places chipped out of the yellow crystal look as if they'd fit your fingertips and toes. You grab a handhold and start to climb.

As soon as you touch the crystal, an enormous pulse of yellow light flashes out from the crystal's center and washes over you. Suddenly a hole opens up in the crystal, and brilliant ribbons of golden energy start whirling around its edges.

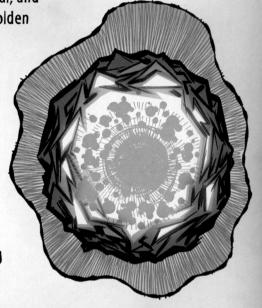

And the energy ribbons start *pulling* at you!

"Are you okay in there?" you hear Miss Fitch calling to you. "Can you get out?"

"There's something weird going on!" you shout. "I don't know what's happening!"

As you watch, the center of the hole in the crystal grows darker and darker . . . until you realize you're looking *through* the strange hole to some other place entirely. It's a window or even a doorway—

—and then it pulls you right in!

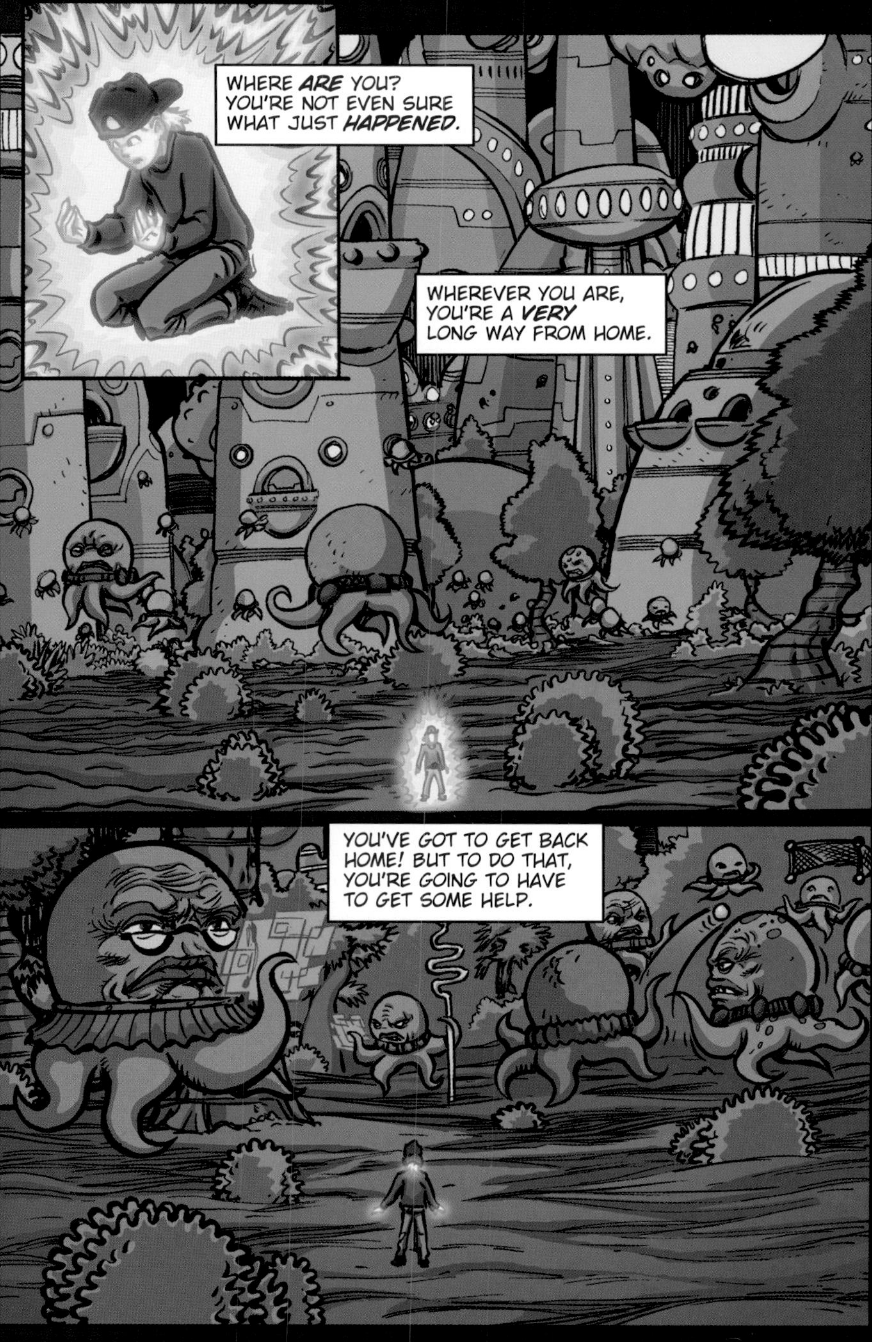
WHERE ARE YOU? YOU'RE NOT EVEN SURE WHAT JUST HAPPENED.
WHEREVER YOU ARE, YOU'RE A VERY LONG WAY FROM HOME.
YOU'VE GOT TO GET BACK HOME! BUT TO DO THAT, YOU'RE GOING TO HAVE TO GET SOME HELP.

GO ON TO THE NEXT PAGE.

TWISTED JOURNEYS®

. . . No matter how *weird* and *huge* these people are, you've got to talk to somebody.

WILL YOU . . .

. . . try to attract the attention of the game players?

TURN TO PAGE 83.

. . . go talk to the alien who's reading a book by himself?

TURN TO PAGE 25.

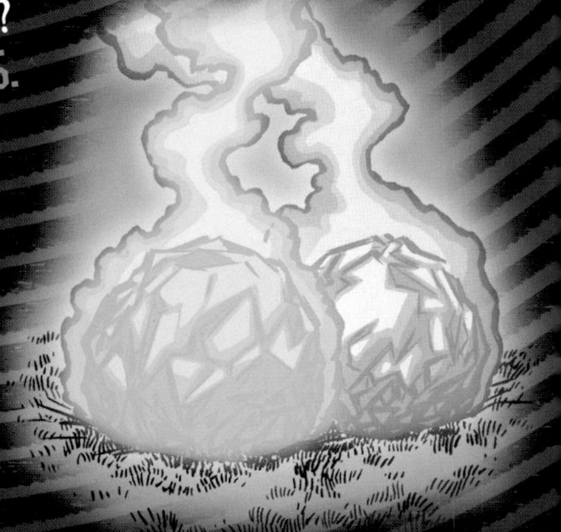

From that day forward, your life takes a serious turn for the dramatic. Now that the ability to turn into a giant is yours to command, the possibilities are endless!

You could establish a one-person demolition company and knock down buildings all day.

You could start your own traveling sideshow and charge people money just to get a glimpse of you.

You could even have an acting career in giant monster movies.

But what you decide to do is better than all of those put together. Because when you're a giant, no one can recognize you. It's the perfect secret identity. So you become . . .

. . . *Kolossal Kid!* The world's youngest, biggest superhero!

You even get your mom to help you make a huge "K" logo that you pin to your giant shirt.

Look out, world! Here comes Kolossal Kid!

THE END

You don't like the looks of the water down here. Who knows what could be in that stuff? You'll just stay on this box and see where it goes.

It's not long before you start to regret that decision, though. The tunnel you're traveling down gets darker . . . and darker . . . and even darker. The water starts to flow faster too. "Maybe I ought to try to make it to the side," you murmur . . . but then you spot something shining over near a wall. Something glimmering and red.

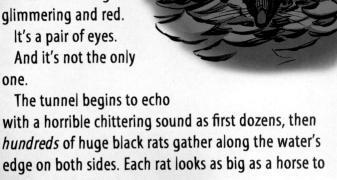

It's a pair of eyes.

And it's not the only one.

The tunnel begins to echo with a horrible chittering sound as first dozens, then *hundreds* of huge black rats gather along the water's edge on both sides. Each rat looks as big as a horse to you . . .

. . . and then, one by one, they slip into the water and start swimming toward you, sharp teeth gleaming . . .

THE END

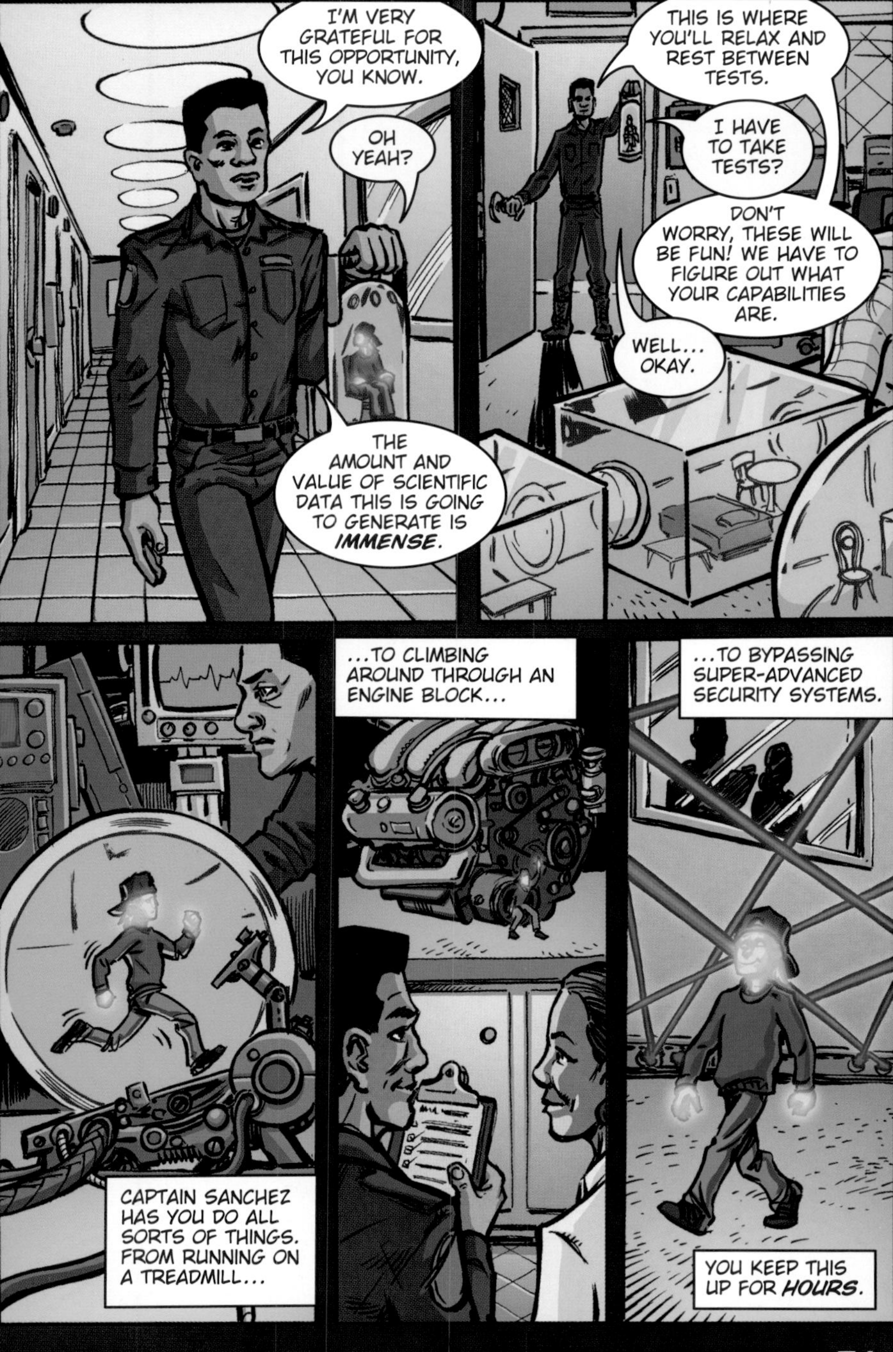
I'M VERY GRATEFUL FOR THIS OPPORTUNITY, YOU KNOW.
OH YEAH?
THE AMOUNT AND VALUE OF SCIENTIFIC DATA THIS IS GOING TO GENERATE IS *IMMENSE*.
THIS IS WHERE YOU'LL RELAX AND REST BETWEEN TESTS.
I HAVE TO TAKE TESTS?
DON'T WORRY, THESE WILL BE FUN! WE HAVE TO FIGURE OUT WHAT YOUR CAPABILITIES ARE.
WELL... OKAY.
CAPTAIN SANCHEZ HAS YOU DO ALL SORTS OF THINGS. FROM RUNNING ON A TREADMILL...
...TO CLIMBING AROUND THROUGH AN ENGINE BLOCK...
...TO BYPASSING SUPER-ADVANCED SECURITY SYSTEMS.
YOU KEEP THIS UP FOR *HOURS*.

TURN TO PAGE 52.

You don't want anything to do with this kid's wacky homemade cures, but you're not exactly ready to face a whole alien world, either. So, while Frummy has his back turned, you grab a power cord dangling from the edge of the table and slide down it to the floor. You're pretty sure you can hide among all the stuff he's got set up in here.

You scurry across the floor, duck around something shaped like a football (except it's the size of your school bus), and zip down a long, narrow open space between two pieces of what might be cardboard. Behind you, Frummy shouts, "Hey! Where'd you go?"

The time to hide is *now*. You turn a couple of corners . . .

. . . and realize the cardboard walls are part of a maze.

A maze you've just gotten lost in.

GO ON TO THE NEXT PAGE.

You might be able to go back the way you came . . . but you're not sure.

WILL YOU . . .

. . . forge ahead and try to find your way out the other side?
TURN TO PAGE 63.

. . . try to go back to the entrance?
TURN TO PAGE 88.

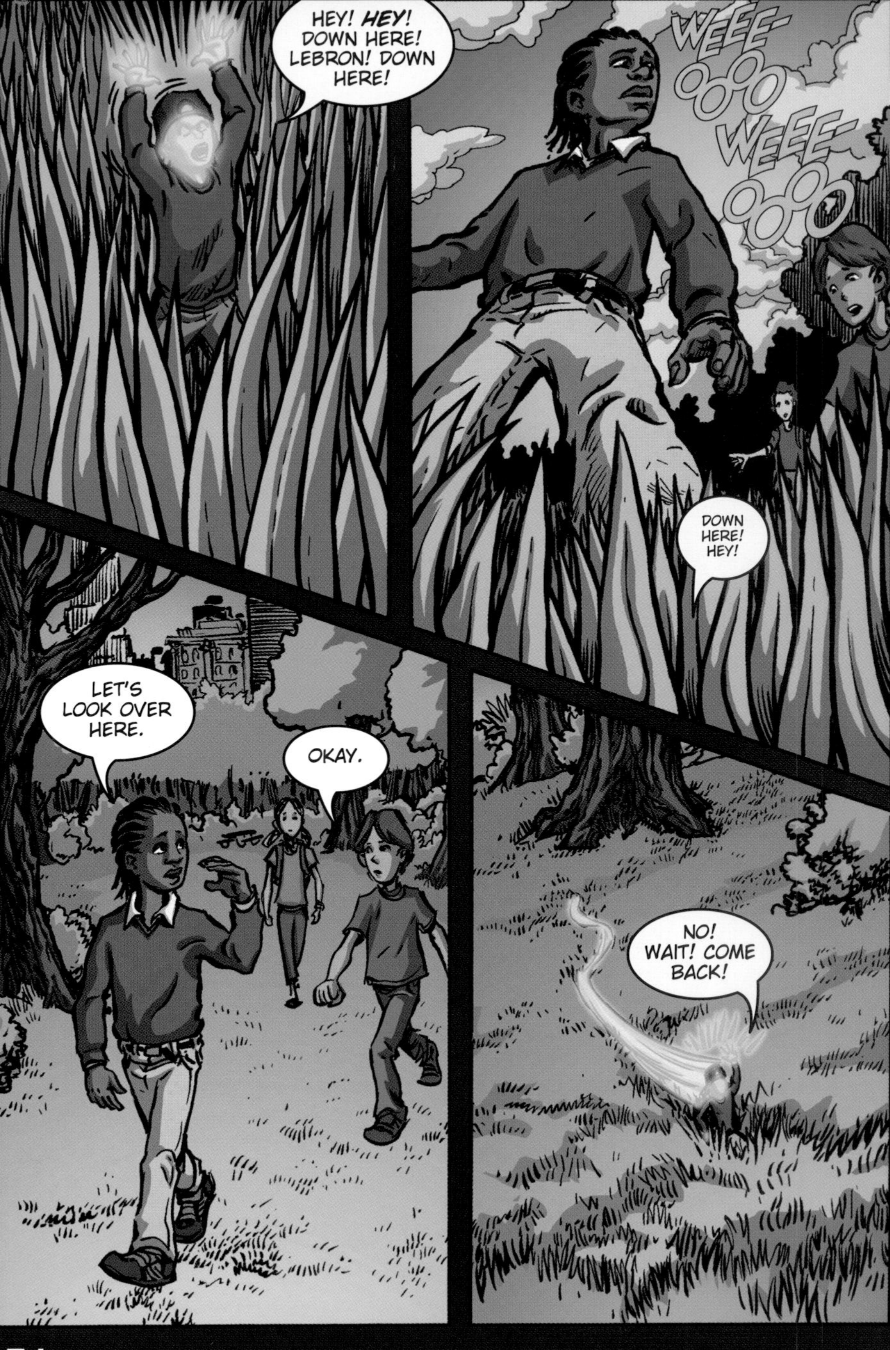
HEY! ***HEY!*** DOWN HERE! LEBRON! DOWN HERE!
WEEE-OOOO WEEE-OOOO
DOWN HERE! HEY!
LET'S LOOK OVER HERE.
OKAY.
NO! WAIT! COME BACK!

Suddenly the whole sky goes dark. For a second, you're confused. You think, *What is this, an eclipse?* Then you realize the sun is blotted out because a *hand* is coming down toward you.

The hand picks you up, and you're being squeezed so hard, you think your rib cage is going to break. Plus, you almost hurl from being jerked straight up into the air so fast! Then you come to a stop, and a wind blasts into your face . . . a wind that smells very strongly of strained peas.

You're in the hands of a two-year-old boy!

"Little!" the boy shrieks, delighted. He wiggles you back and forth as if you were a rag doll, and you're afraid your head's going to come off.

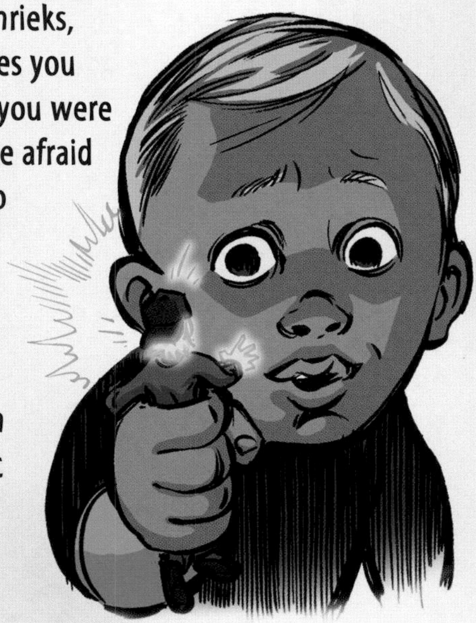

"STOP!" you shout, waving your arms at him. You don't know if he can understand you, but he giggles at the high-pitched sound of your voice.

Then you remember what most two-year-olds do when they see something really, really interesting.

They put the interesting thing in their mouths.

And sure enough, as he gazes at you with wide eyes, the little boy starts bringing you closer and closer to his lips . . . and his mouth opens wide . . .

. . . and an *enormous* hand shoots down and grabs the boy's wrist. You crank your head back to look up at the hand's owner, and relief floods through you as you recognize LeBron.

"Oh no, you don't!" LeBron says. He carefully takes you out of the little boy's grip. "My friend's coming with *me*."

LeBron gently places you in his shirt pocket. All your classmates and friends gather around to get a look. Then Miss Fitch pushes her way through and leans in close.

"I have to get you to the proper authorities," she says. Her voice is so loud it hurts your ears.

GO ON TO THE NEXT PAGE.

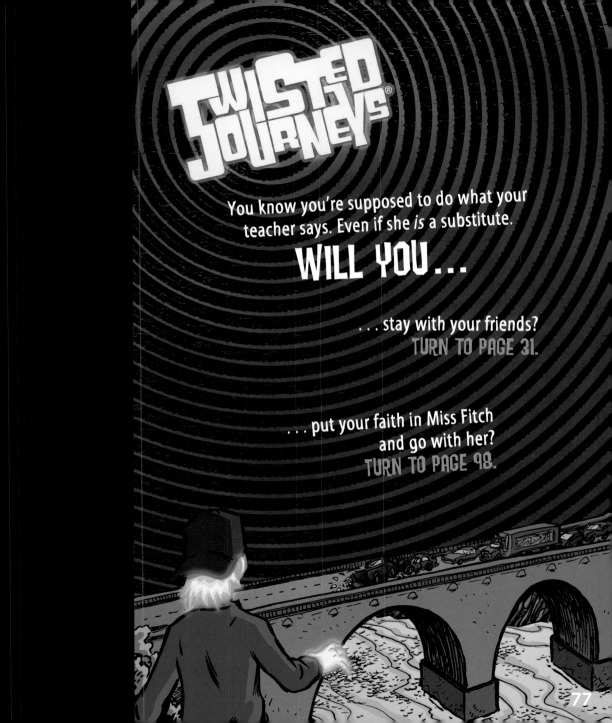

TWISTED JOURNEYS®

You know you're supposed to do what your teacher says. Even if she *is* a substitute.

WILL YOU...

...stay with your friends?
TURN TO PAGE 31.

...put your faith in Miss Fitch and go with her?
TURN TO PAGE 98.

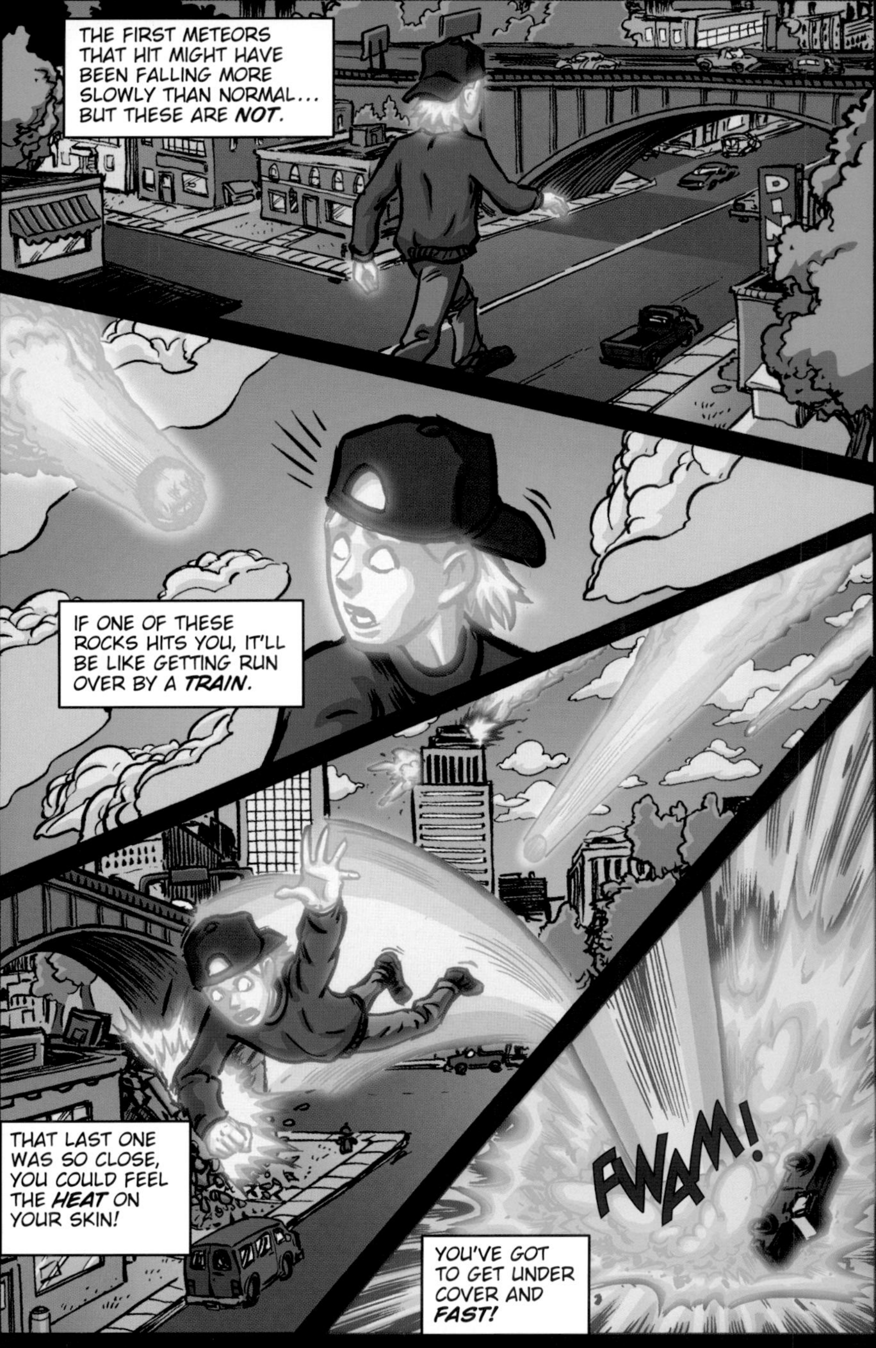
THE FIRST METEORS THAT HIT MIGHT HAVE BEEN FALLING MORE SLOWLY THAN NORMAL... BUT THESE ARE *NOT*.
IF ONE OF THESE ROCKS HITS YOU, IT'LL BE LIKE GETTING RUN OVER BY A *TRAIN*.
THAT LAST ONE WAS SO CLOSE, YOU COULD FEEL THE *HEAT* ON YOUR SKIN!
FWAM!
YOU'VE GOT TO GET UNDER COVER AND *FAST!*

GO ON TO THE NEXT PAGE.

You can't take the chance of getting punched full of holes—those meteors could kill you! You'd better take cover and wait for the storm to pass.

You're so huge, it's a bit of a tight fit, but you squeeze yourself under the overpass and cover your head with your hands. You can hear the whistling sound of an approaching meteor—

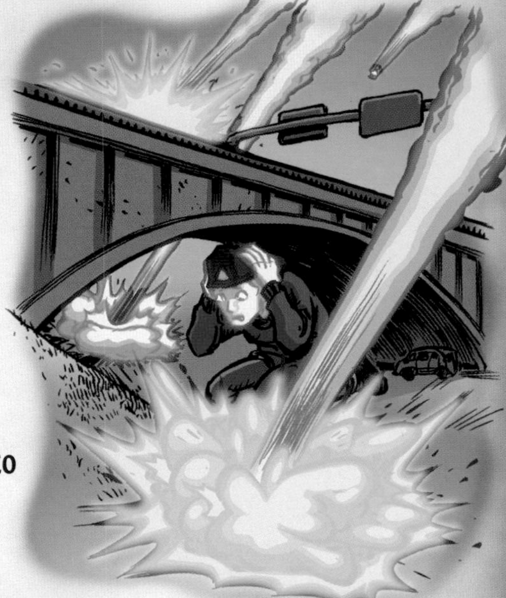

—and it smashes into the bridge right above your head! Concrete dust rains down around you.

Slam! Another meteor crashes into the bridge. *Slam, slam, slam!* A few meteors punch through, crashing into the ground below.

A van comes screeching to a halt near your feet, its owners desperate for shelter from the storm.

Impact after impact, crash after crash, the bridge starts to fall to pieces. And then . . .

. . . it all stops.

And one yellow, glowing crystal rolls to a stop against your right foot.

TURN TO PAGE 105.

You're pretty sure a science exhibit will be safer for you than whatever the "Crazy Cyclones" are. You get comfortable in the alien girl's bag and just ride along as she floats off the blimp and heads into the park.

She goes to a building filled from top to bottom with insane-looking alien machines. You hear people talk about devices called "thought tasters" and others called "gravity swirlers," and you can't make heads or tails out of any of it.

But then the girl floats over into a different room and lets out a squeal.

"Oh, cool!" she says. "Look how it *glows!*"

Glows? Huh? You shift around in the bag to get a better look—

—and there, inside a glass display case, is a huge yellow crystal just like the one that brought you here!

GO ON TO THE NEXT PAGE.

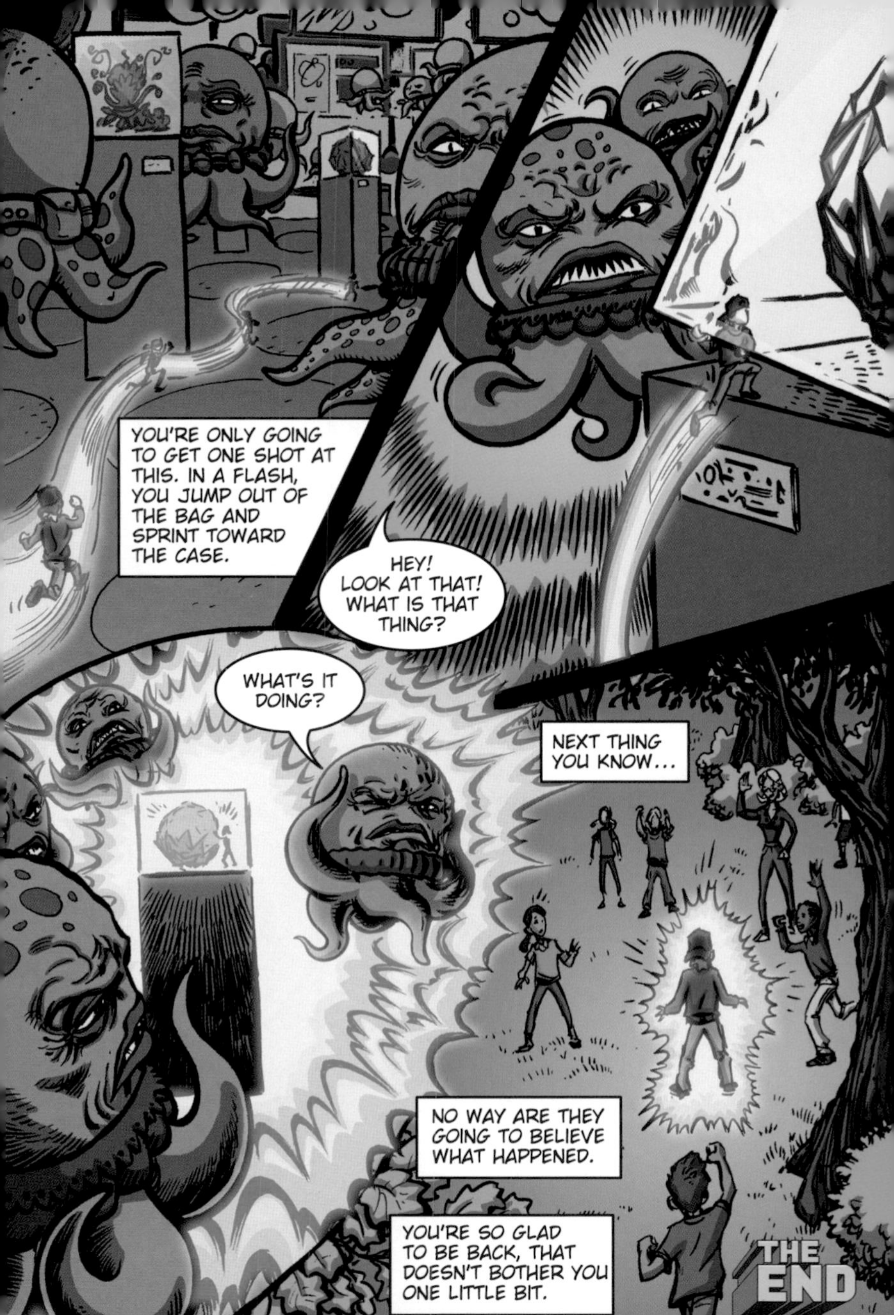
YOU'RE ONLY GOING TO GET ONE SHOT AT THIS. IN A FLASH, YOU JUMP OUT OF THE BAG AND SPRINT TOWARD THE CASE.
HEY! LOOK AT THAT! WHAT IS THAT THING?
WHAT'S IT DOING?
NEXT THING YOU KNOW...
NO WAY ARE THEY GOING TO BELIEVE WHAT HAPPENED.
YOU'RE SO GLAD TO BE BACK, THAT DOESN'T BOTHER YOU ONE LITTLE BIT.
THE END

You've got to think fast!

"W-w-well, there's no need to fight," you tell the three-eyed giant. "If you come on all strong and get ugly about it, then, uh . . . then . . . uh . . ."

He taps his foot impatiently. "Yes? Then what?"

"Then we won't cook our incredibly tasty food for you!" You're sweating—you know this is the longest of long shots—but it was all you could come up with.

But, wait! He's interested! "Tasty food, you say? Hmmm. The food on our planet *is* awfully bland. And you think if we *didn't* invade, your people might cook this wonderful food for us?"

"I'm sure some sort of peaceful, reasonable, food-based agreement can be reached," you tell him.

And the negotiations go from there. Instead of conquerors, the giants soon become enthusiastic restaurant patrons.

Maybe you're stuck as a 70-foot-tall glowing giant . . . but at least you saved the planet!

THE END

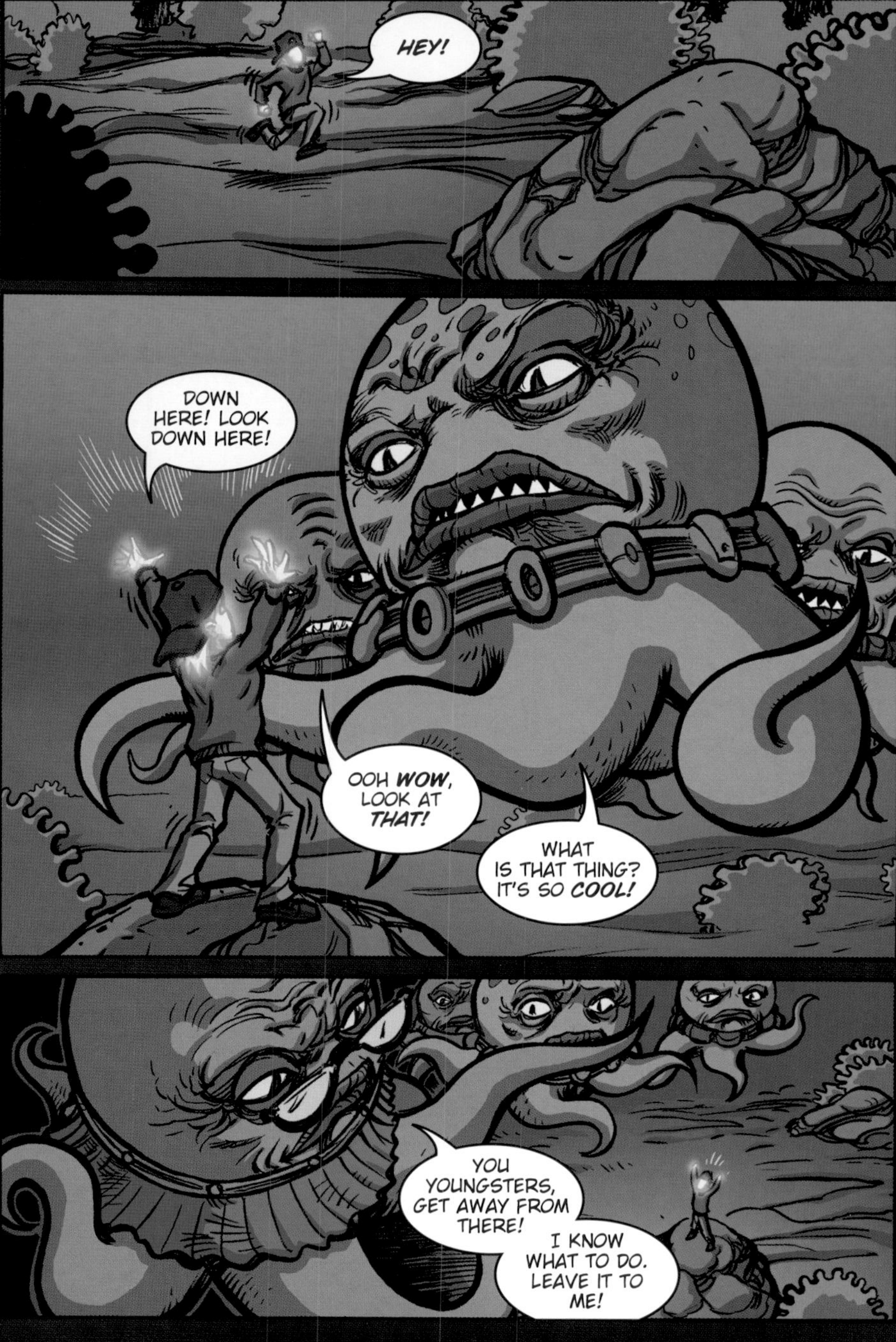
HEY!
DOWN HERE! LOOK DOWN HERE!
OOH **WOW**, LOOK AT **THAT!**
WHAT IS THAT THING? IT'S SO **COOL!**
YOU YOUNGSTERS, GET AWAY FROM THERE!
I KNOW WHAT TO DO. LEAVE IT TO ME!

GO ON TO THE NEXT PAGE.

Kids seem to be kids, whether they're human or giant weird aliens, and you might like to get to know these ones. But maybe going with a grown-up would be smarter.

WILL YOU...

. . . go with the group of kids?
TURN TO PAGE 12.

. . . go with the old lady?
TURN TO PAGE 91.

You reason that if you head to that construction site, you'll probably be able to get a good look all around you, so you leave the trees and head that way.

And you were right. When you get up to the top of the hill, you have a fantastic view of the city below you and all the surrounding countryside. What you didn't expect was someone on the sixth floor of the unfinished building to lean out and say, "Hey! Hey, you! Giant glowy thing!"

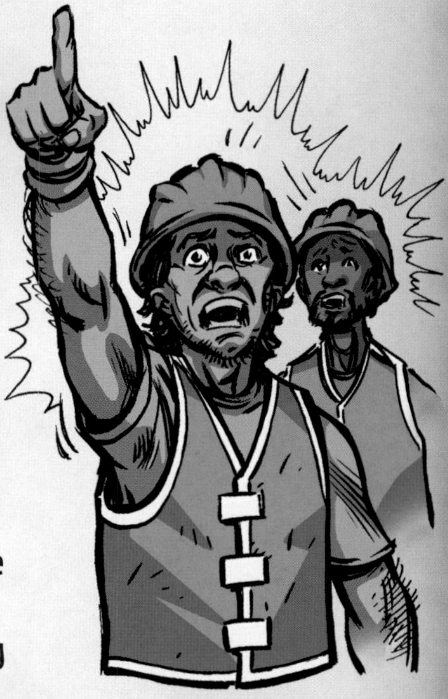

You look around and see a handful of construction workers. They're all staring at you. "What? Are you talking to me?"

"Yes, we're talking to you!" one of them shouts. "You've gotta do something! Those meteors are gonna wreck the whole city! You've gotta stop 'em!"

Stop the meteors? "How?"

He points at a huge wrecking ball. "Use that!"

GO ON TO THE NEXT PAGE.

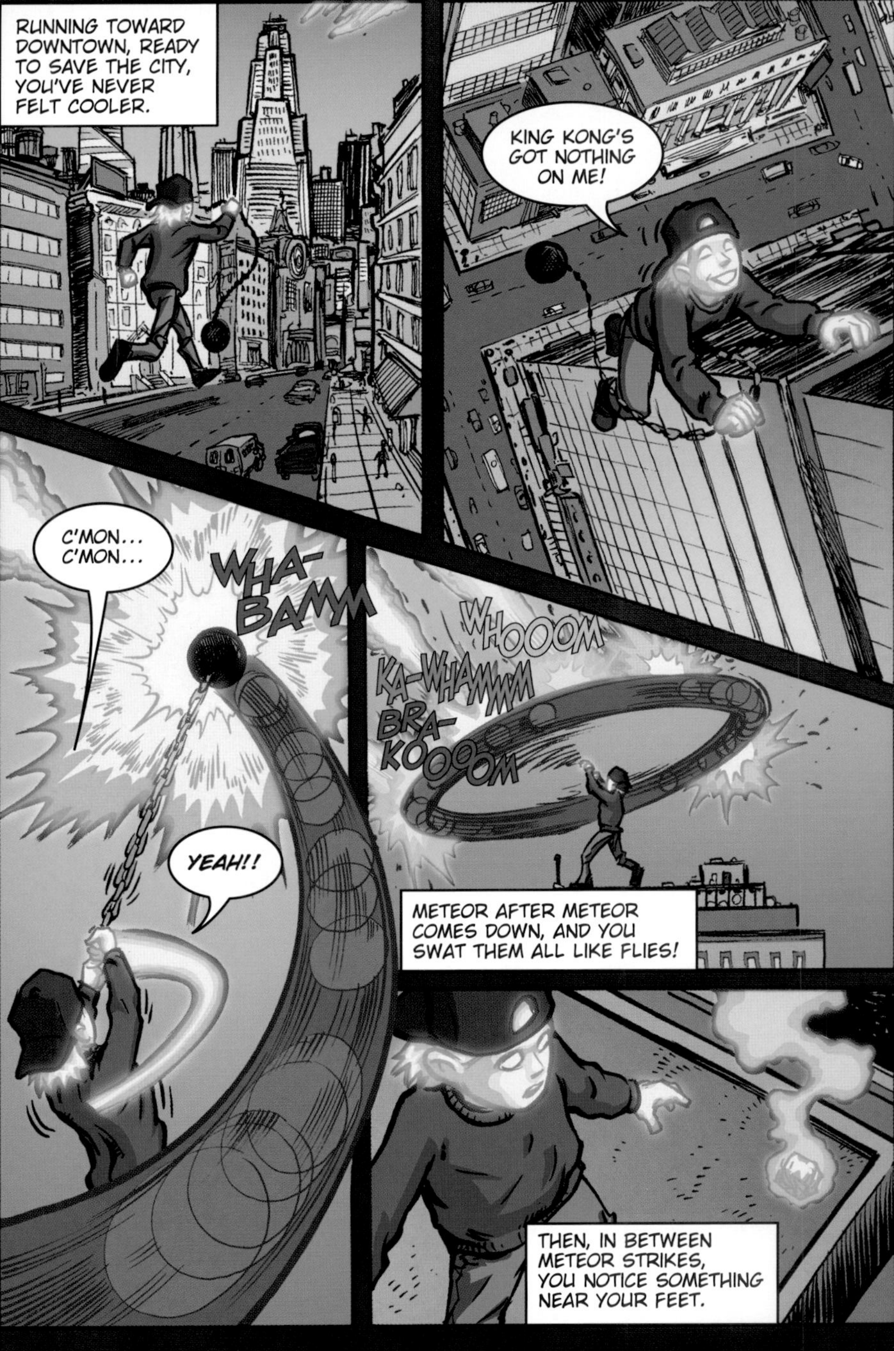
RUNNING TOWARD DOWNTOWN, READY TO SAVE THE CITY, YOU'VE NEVER FELT COOLER.
KING KONG'S GOT NOTHING ON ME!
C'MON... C'MON...
WHA-BAMM
YEAH!!
WHOOOM
KA-WHAMMM
BRA-KOOOOM
METEOR AFTER METEOR COMES DOWN, AND YOU SWAT THEM ALL LIKE FLIES!
THEN, IN BETWEEN METEOR STRIKES, YOU NOTICE SOMETHING NEAR YOUR FEET.

TURN TO PAGE 97.

“Okay,” you tell LeBron. “If you want to try it too, c’mon, let’s go.”

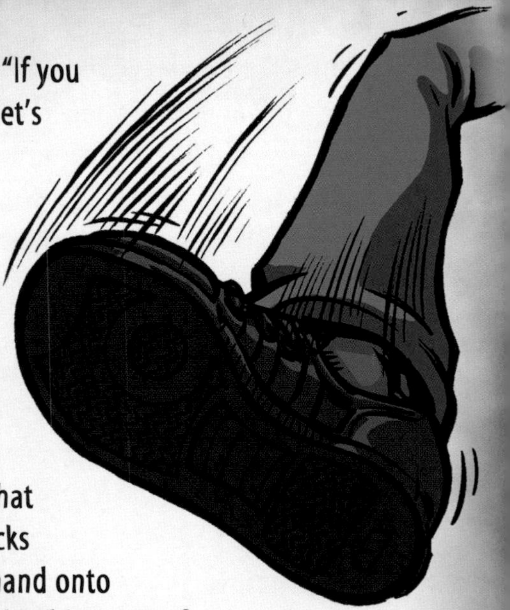

Laughing with excitement, LeBron and the rest of your friends rush back over to the crystals. Miss Fitch is there, trying to tell some police officers and firefighters what happened, but LeBron ducks around her and slaps his hand onto the green crystal. Right behind him, six of your other classmates zip in and do the same.

Instantly, LeBron starts to shrink. In a few seconds, you and LeBron and your other friends are all about an inch tall, standing there amid the towering blades of grass.

“Wow!” LeBron shouts. “It’s even cooler than I thought it would be!”

But then you hear a roaring sound from above you, and you realize it’s *words*. A man is yelling, “Everybody get back! Get away!” The ground starts to shake as colossal footsteps pound toward you . . .

. . . and the last thing you see is the bottom of a police officer’s shoe—a shoe the size of a *house*—as it comes down right on top of you.

THE END

You want no part of this maze or Frummy the giant floating nerd or this whole huge weird dimension. You head back the way you came . . .

. . . except you've made a wrong turn somewhere. "Don't run!" Frummy shouts from outside the maze. "I just want to find out what you are!"

"Get away from me!" you shout back and break into a sprint. You turn a corner, and without warning, you're falling off the edge of a table! When you land, you're lying on a wire framework above what looks like a big array of bizarre alien batteries.

"Don't move. The batteries are dangerous!" Frummy says, sending a couple of wriggling tentacles toward you. "You'll make such a great science project!" But then he bumps the maze, toppling you off the wires.

Electricity courses through you. Despite Frummy's best efforts, this is . . .

THE END

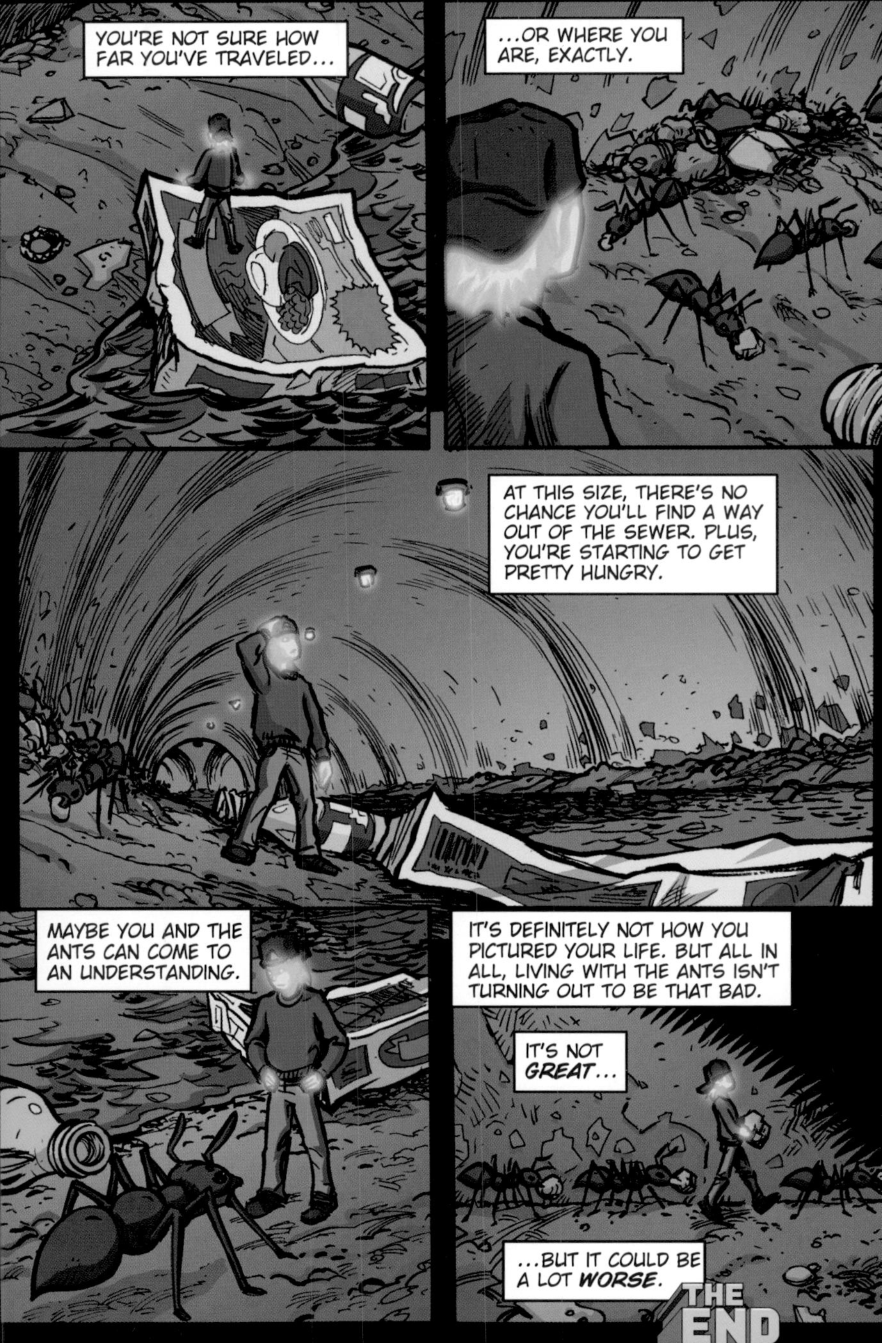
YOU'RE NOT SURE HOW FAR YOU'VE TRAVELED...
...OR WHERE YOU ARE, EXACTLY.
AT THIS SIZE, THERE'S NO CHANCE YOU'LL FIND A WAY OUT OF THE SEWER. PLUS, YOU'RE STARTING TO GET PRETTY HUNGRY.
MAYBE YOU AND THE ANTS CAN COME TO AN UNDERSTANDING.
IT'S DEFINITELY NOT HOW YOU PICTURED YOUR LIFE. BUT ALL IN ALL, LIVING WITH THE ANTS ISN'T TURNING OUT TO BE THAT BAD.
IT'S NOT *GREAT*...
...BUT IT COULD BE A LOT ***WORSE***.
THE END

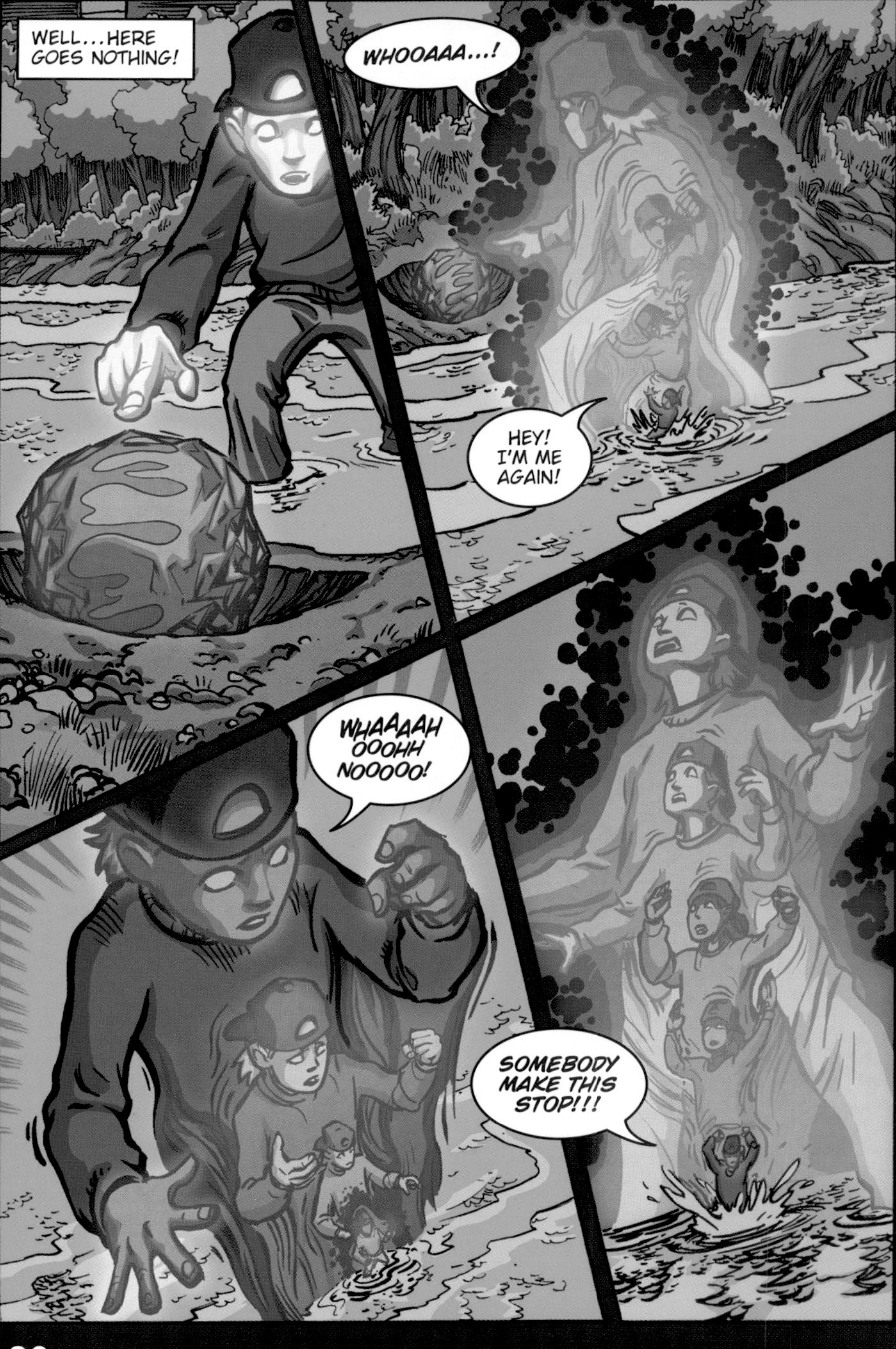
WELL...HERE GOES NOTHING!
WHOOAAA...!
HEY! I'M ME AGAIN!
WHAAAAH OOOHH NOOOOO!
SOMEBODY MAKE THIS STOP!!!

TURN TO PAGE 47.

"Oh, dearie me!" the gigantic old lady says. "We need to get you somewhere safe! It's a good thing I don't live far from here."

"You've got to help me!" you tell her. "I'm not from this world! I've got to get home!"

The old lady takes you into her house. Everything in here is just as strange as it is outside—all the furniture is shaped like big bowls, to fit the aliens' round bodies.

"I know you're not from here, dear," she says. "This happens every so often. Some tiny little person just shows up. *Pop!*"

You weren't expecting that! "So what happens to them? How do they get home?"

"Oh, they don't get home," she says sadly. "I'm afraid it's a one-way trip. But don't worry! I'll keep you here with me. Nice and safe. Plus, it will be so nice to have someone to talk to!"

GO ON TO THE NEXT PAGE.

TWISTED JOURNEYS®

This alien lady seems nice enough, but you doubt she can help you get home.

WILL YOU . . .

. . . stay here with the woman?
TURN TO PAGE 15.

. . . try to escape from her house?
TURN TO PAGE 102.

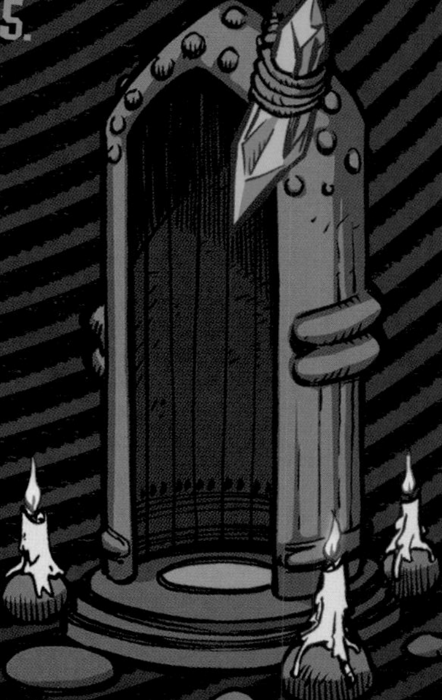

And suddenly—there aren't any more meteors.

You look around, the wrecking ball ready in your hands, but . . . the meteor storm has stopped. Suddenly you feel very self-conscious, standing there on the roof.

Then you're bathed in light, as multiple spotlights hit you, and you realize half a dozen news helicopters are homing in on you. You drop the wrecking ball and shield your eyes.

"That was amazing!" someone says over a loudspeaker. "Thank you! Thank you so much!"

"Uh . . . " You're not sure what to say. "You're welcome?"

The helicopters land, and reporters flood out of them. They all want to talk to you . . . so you sit down on the roof and have a chat with them.

The next day, headlines everywhere say: GIANT GLOWING HERO SAVES CITY!

The whole country *loves* you. You get tons of awards, tons of recognition . . .

. . . and you decide that being a giant might not be too bad at all.

THE END

You've always wondered what it would be like to go on a rampage, like the ones you've seen in monster movies. And that guy with the loudspeaker is *really* obnoxious.

"Monster irritated!" you bellow, and the sound of your voice makes all the trees nearby sway and tremble. A few of the cops' hats fly off their heads. "Monster de*stroy!*"

Leaning down, you pick up one of the cop cars (after making sure there's no one inside—you don't want to hurt anybody) and fling it as hard as you can. The car arcs across the countryside and splashes down in the middle of a lake about a mile away. You giggle as the guy with the loudspeaker yelps and runs away.

You stomp around a little, just to see how it feels. The ground shakes hard enough to break some windows. This is fun!

GO ON TO THE NEXT PAGE.

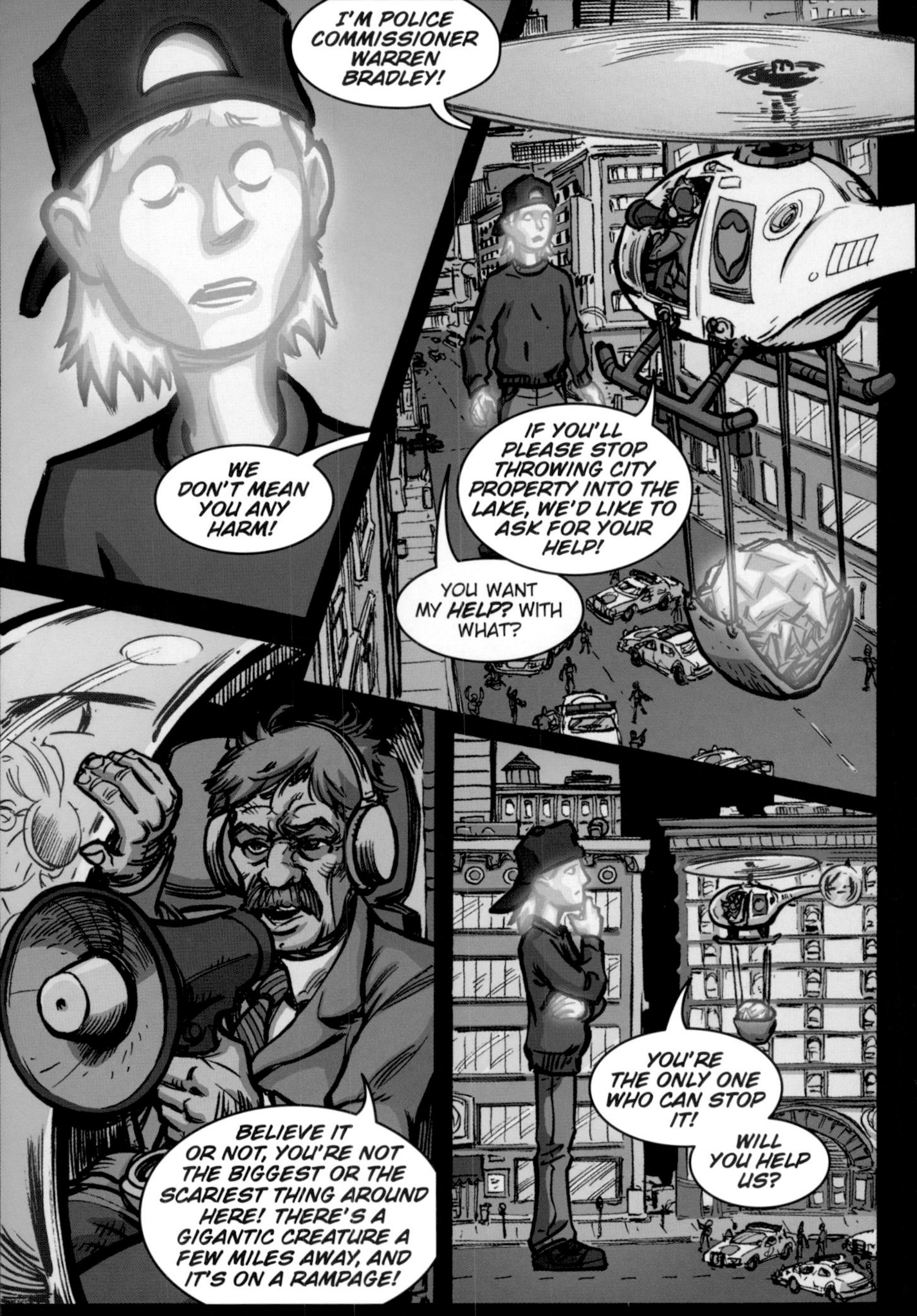
I'M POLICE COMMISSIONER WARREN BRADLEY!
WE DON'T MEAN YOU ANY HARM!
IF YOU'LL PLEASE STOP THROWING CITY PROPERTY INTO THE LAKE, WE'D LIKE TO ASK FOR YOUR HELP!
YOU WANT MY *HELP?* WITH WHAT?
BELIEVE IT OR NOT, YOU'RE NOT THE BIGGEST OR THE SCARIEST THING AROUND HERE! THERE'S A GIGANTIC CREATURE A FEW MILES AWAY, AND IT'S ON A RAMPAGE!
YOU'RE THE ONLY ONE WHO CAN STOP IT!
WILL YOU HELP US?

TURN TO PAGE 9.

Gross spider-lizard or not, it still topples over just fine when you ram into it with your shoulder. Before it has a chance to set itself right, you grab one of its eight legs and start spinning it around.

The creature snarls and tries to bite you, but it can't quite reach you as it spins. Then you let it go—and it follows the police car right into the lake.

Apparently weird giant mutant spider-lizards don't like water. It shrieks and flails its limbs and tries to swim . . .

. . . and then it dissolves into a huge mass of disgusting spider goo.

"Great work!" the commissioner says, flying up to you in the helicopter.

"Thanks," you reply. "But I don't know what to do now! I'm not normally this big!"

As more yellow meteors streak across the sky, the commissioner says, "I think I can put you to good use . . ."

THE END

TWISTED JOURNEYS®

There's another yellow crystal . . .
just like the one that got you into this mess.

WILL YOU . . .

. . . take a chance, touch the crystal, and hope it turns you back into your normal self?

TURN TO PAGE 27.

. . . leave the crystal alone, stay a giant, and avoid any *more* possible weirdness?

TURN TO PAGE 93.

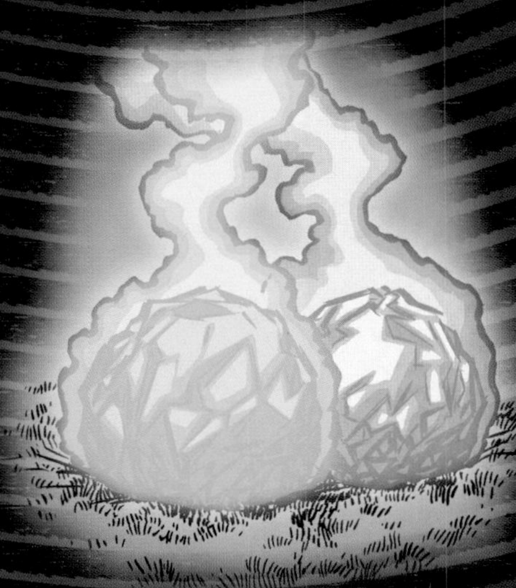

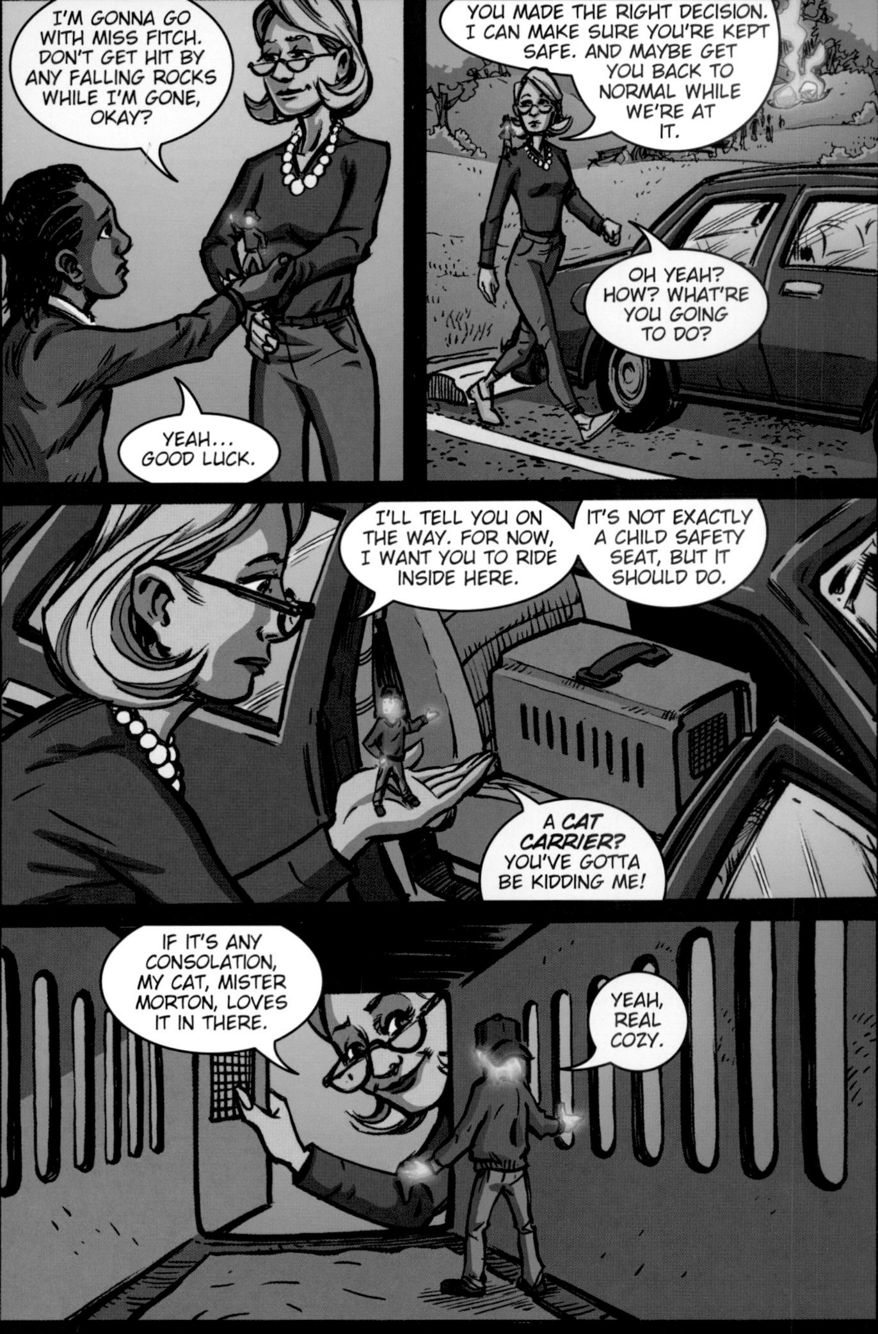
I'M GONNA GO WITH MISS FITCH. DON'T GET HIT BY ANY FALLING ROCKS WHILE I'M GONE, OKAY?
YEAH... GOOD LUCK.
YOU MADE THE RIGHT DECISION. I CAN MAKE SURE YOU'RE KEPT SAFE. AND MAYBE GET YOU BACK TO NORMAL WHILE WE'RE AT IT.
OH YEAH? HOW? WHAT'RE YOU GOING TO DO?
I'LL TELL YOU ON THE WAY. FOR NOW, I WANT YOU TO RIDE INSIDE HERE.
IT'S NOT EXACTLY A CHILD SAFETY SEAT, BUT IT SHOULD DO.
A *CAT CARRIER?* YOU'VE GOTTA BE KIDDING ME!
IF IT'S ANY CONSOLATION, MY CAT, MISTER MORTON, LOVES IT IN THERE.
YEAH, REAL COZY.

GO ON TO THE NEXT PAGE.

You're not sure where Miss Fitch is taking you, so you don't know how long the ride will be. You figure you might as well make some conversation.

"Have you ever seen anything like those meteors before?" you ask.

She shakes her head. "No. Normally, if a meteor that big fell out of the sky and hit the ground, there'd be enough kinetic energy released to flatten half the city. But these things came down *slowly*."

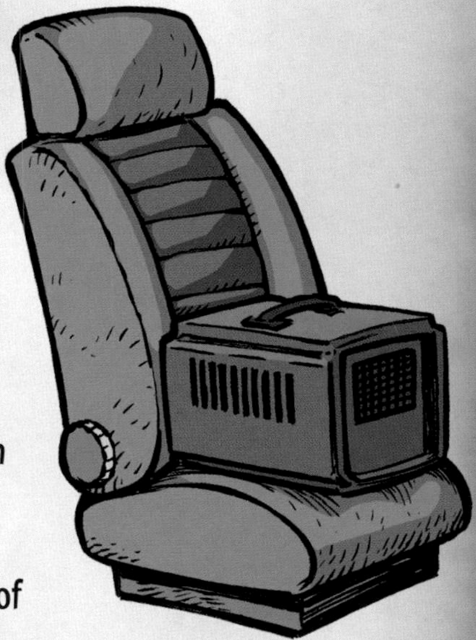

You follow what she's saying, more or less, and you're very glad you've been paying attention in science class. "So—what? Do you think they're . . . some kind of alien rocks or something?"

She shrugs. "I don't know. We're going to talk to some people who might have an idea."

Miss Fitch falls silent and doesn't seem to want to talk at all now.

You look around. The carrier doesn't smell too good. You think you could climb out of it pretty easily.

GO ON TO THE NEXT PAGE.

"Now, hang on a minute, here," you say, as a few things occur to you. "Giant rocks just fell out of the sky and almost crushed us all—never mind what's happened to *me*. How come you're taking me away somewhere? Shouldn't you have waited for the police or called all our parents or something?"

"You're pretty smart," Miss Fitch says. "And yes, you're right. This is what you'd call 'nonstandard.' You see, I'm not really a substitute teacher."

Huh? "You're not?"

"No. I was sent to your school because some of our scientists had figured out that those strange meteors might land somewhere close by. If they did, I was supposed to observe."

You don't know what to make of that. "So . . . who do you work for?"

"A government agency."

"You're a *secret agent?* No way!"

She smiles.

GO ON TO THE NEXT PAGE.

TWISTED JOURNEYS®

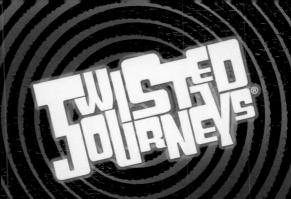

If Miss Fitch is really a secret agent, that would be *so cool!* But what's she going to do with you?

WILL YOU . . .

. . . try to climb out of the carrier and see where you're going?
TURN TO PAGE 10.

. . . stay put and cooperate with her?
TURN TO PAGE 36.

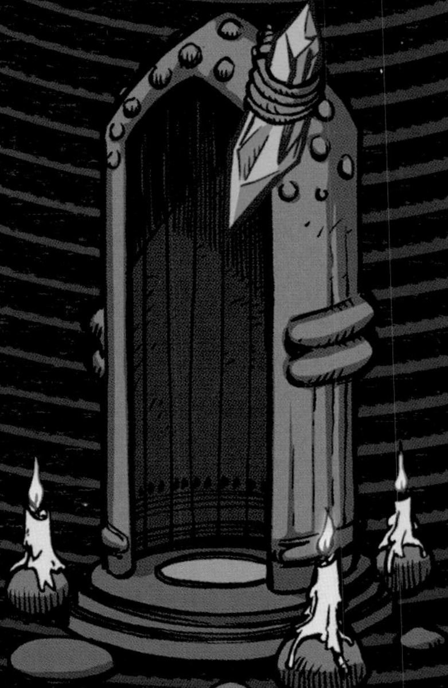

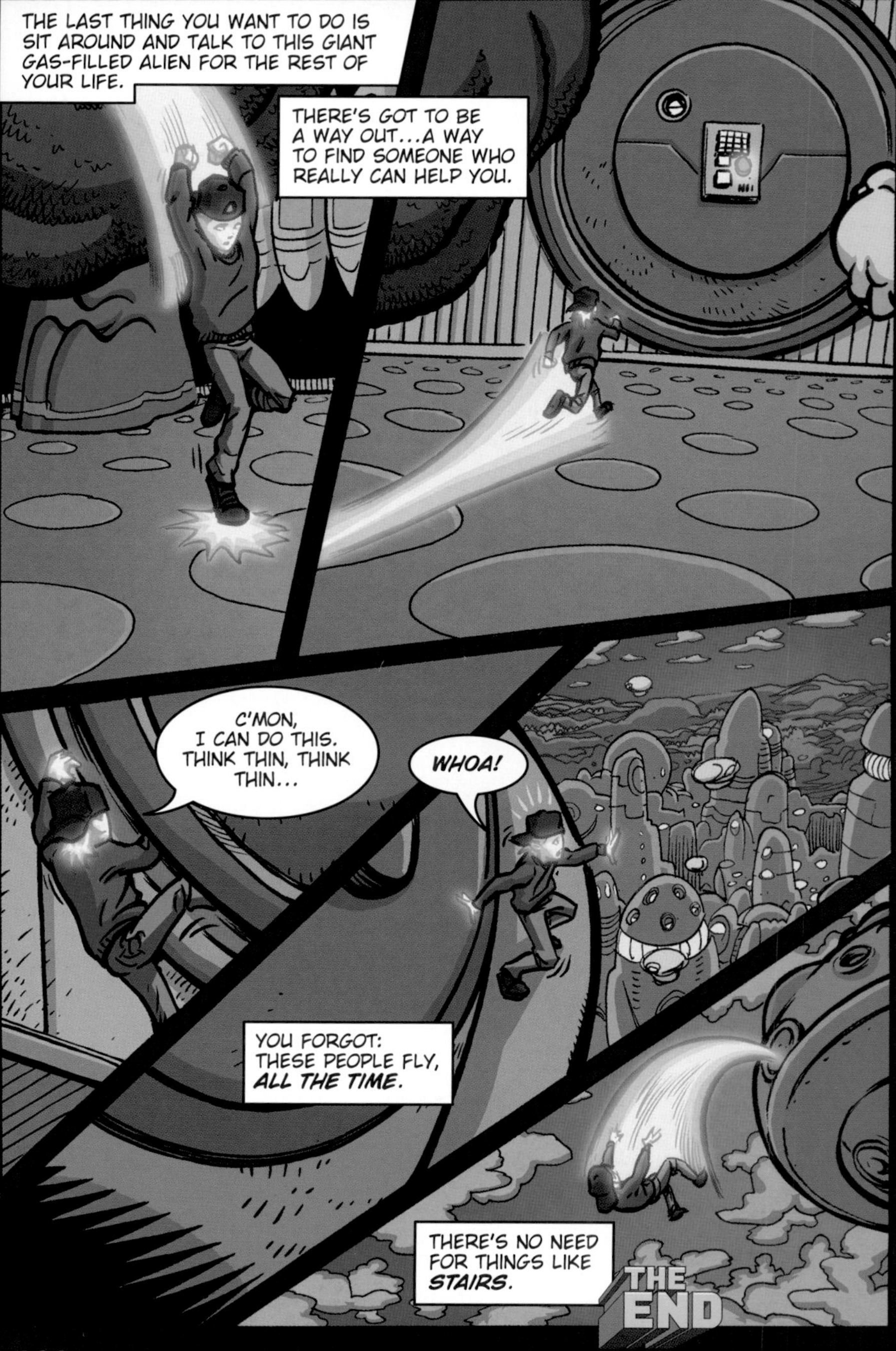
THE LAST THING YOU WANT TO DO IS SIT AROUND AND TALK TO THIS GIANT GAS-FILLED ALIEN FOR THE REST OF YOUR LIFE.
THERE'S GOT TO BE A WAY OUT...A WAY TO FIND SOMEONE WHO REALLY CAN HELP YOU.
C'MON, I CAN DO THIS. THINK THIN, THINK THIN...
WHOA!
YOU FORGOT: THESE PEOPLE FLY, ALL THE TIME.
THERE'S NO NEED FOR THINGS LIKE STAIRS.
THE END

You look up at Major Green thoughtfully. "Y'know, I know you're trying to help. Everyone is . . . but . . ."

She kneels down and looks you in the eye. "What's on your mind?"

"Well, it's just that nothing like this has ever happened to me before. What if I want to, y'know, *stay* like this for a while? Isn't there something useful I could do?"

Slowly, Major Green breaks out into a smile. "Why, yes," she says. "Yes, I believe there is something you can do if you want to remain the size you are now. Let me make a phone call."

She leaves the room but comes back about five minutes later. "There's someone you should meet," she tells you, and holds up your transportation case.

Major Green takes you for another car ride. You end up downtown, surrounded by huge skyscrapers, and she takes you into one of them.

GO ON TO THE NEXT PAGE.

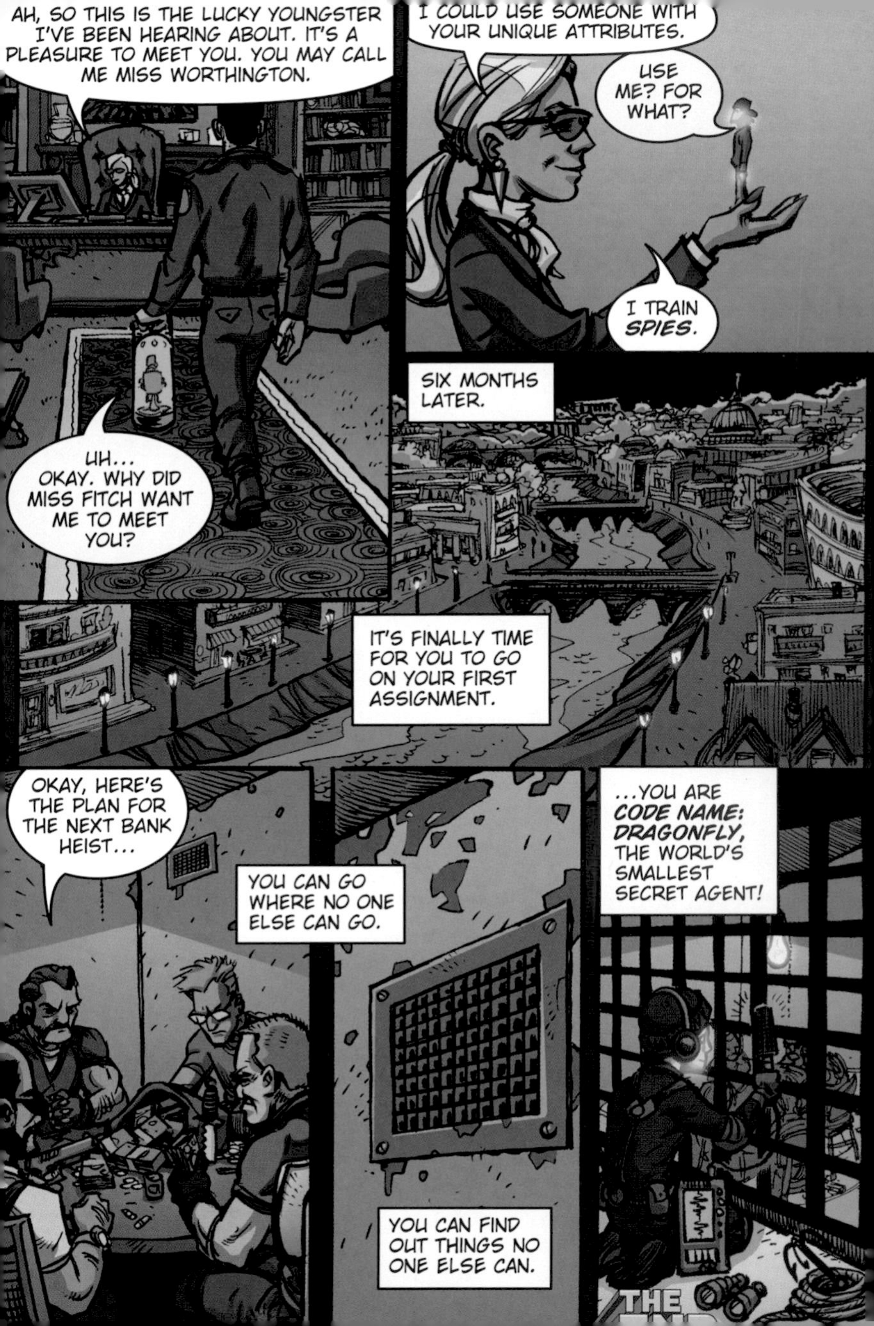
AH, SO THIS IS THE LUCKY YOUNGSTER I'VE BEEN HEARING ABOUT. IT'S A PLEASURE TO MEET YOU. YOU MAY CALL ME MISS WORTHINGTON.
UH... OKAY. WHY DID MISS FITCH WANT ME TO MEET YOU?
I COULD USE SOMEONE WITH YOUR UNIQUE ATTRIBUTES.
USE ME? FOR WHAT?
I TRAIN *SPIES*.
SIX MONTHS LATER.
IT'S FINALLY TIME FOR YOU TO GO ON YOUR FIRST ASSIGNMENT.
OKAY, HERE'S THE PLAN FOR THE NEXT BANK HEIST...
YOU CAN GO WHERE NO ONE ELSE CAN GO.
YOU CAN FIND OUT THINGS NO ONE ELSE CAN.
...YOU ARE ***CODE NAME: DRAGONFLY,*** THE WORLD'S SMALLEST SECRET AGENT!
THE

The golden glow spreads from the crystal to your foot and from there to the rest of your body. In seconds you feel yourself start to shrink . . .

. . . and suddenly you're sitting there on the concrete under the ruined bridge, your normal kid self again! You're feeling pretty good about getting back to normal.

And that lasts for about ten seconds, until you hear the doors slam on the van. A man and woman have gotten out—and the man's holding a camera.

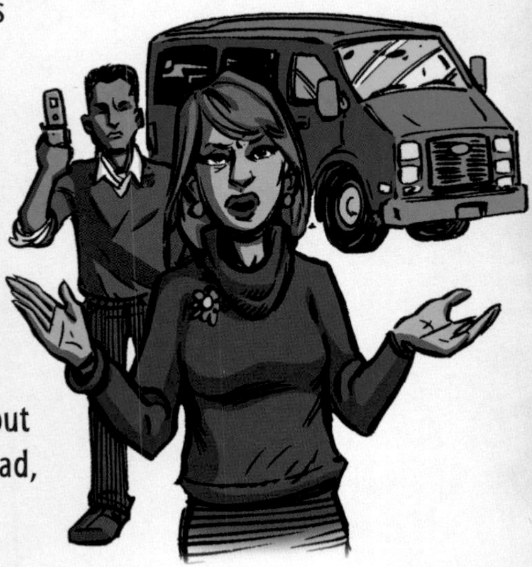

"Why didn't you try to help?" the woman demands.

"Huh?"

"Yeah!" the man says. "You were huge! You could've done something about those meteors! Instead, you just hid down here!"

The woman puts her hands on her hips. "You're going to be in so much trouble! Just wait till we tell your parents!"

Great . . . after all this, now you'll get *grounded*.

THE END

You can move pretty quickly, despite how short your legs are. *Maybe it's because I weigh practically nothing. I wonder if I can jump a long way too?*

It turns out you can. Before the blimp starts to leave, you climb up to the roof of the house and grab a handhold on the blimp. No one notices as you clamber up into the passenger compartment and scurry toward the back.

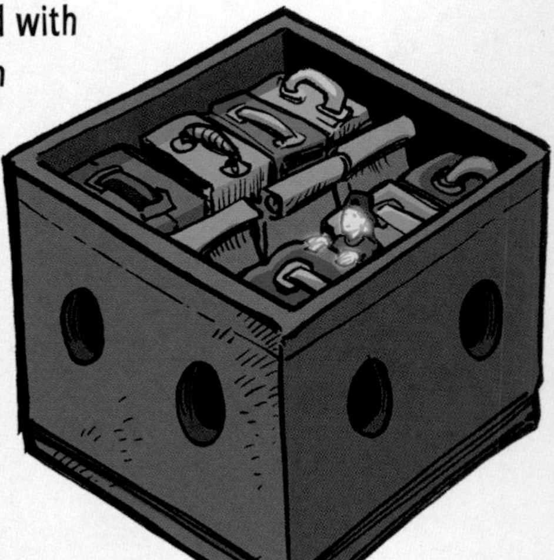

The blimp is packed with round, tentacled alien children. *A field trip?* You know you have to keep out of sight, so when you see a box on the floor in a back corner, you crawl inside.

It's a tight fit, crammed in between smaller boxes and bags of some sort. And something smells kind of good. You're hiding among the lunches!

But when's lunchtime? Maybe it'd be better to move.

GO ON TO THE NEXT PAGE.

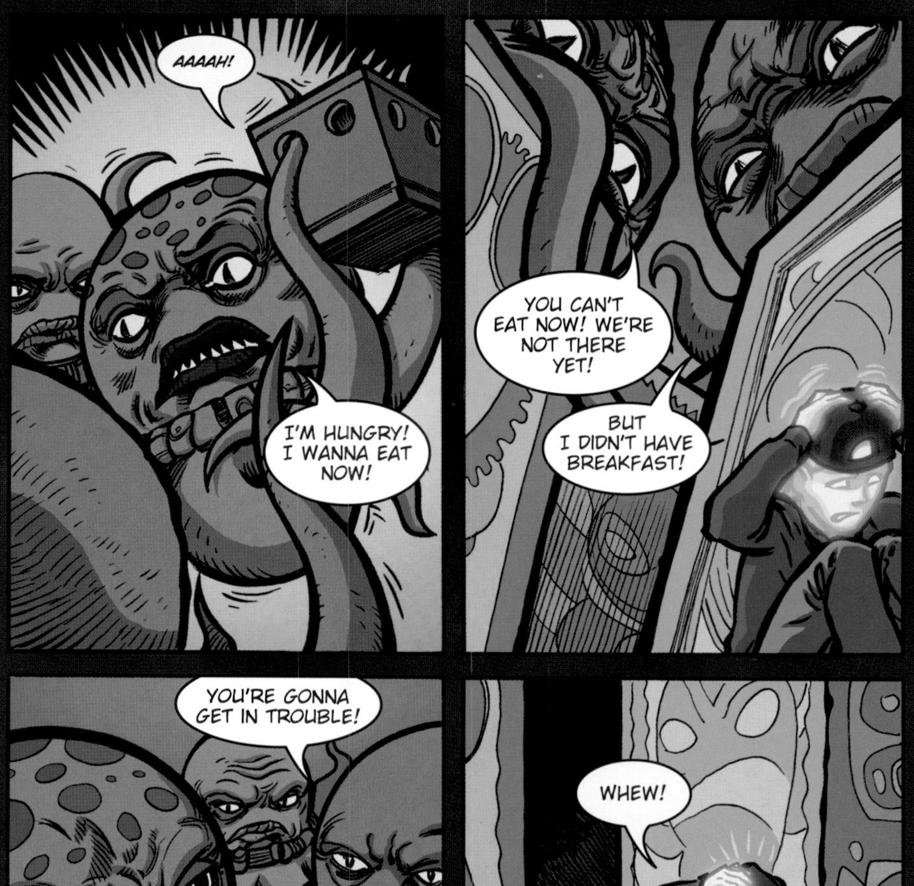
AAAAH!
I'M HUNGRY! I WANNA EAT NOW!
YOU CAN'T EAT NOW! WE'RE NOT THERE YET!
BUT I DIDN'T HAVE BREAKFAST!
YOU'RE GONNA GET IN TROUBLE!
ALL I WANT IS A KRUNKLE BAR! CALM DOWN, WILLYA?
WHEW!
FOR A SECOND, YOU WERE SURE THAT ALIEN KID WAS GOING TO MISTAKE YOU FOR A MIDMORNING SNACK!

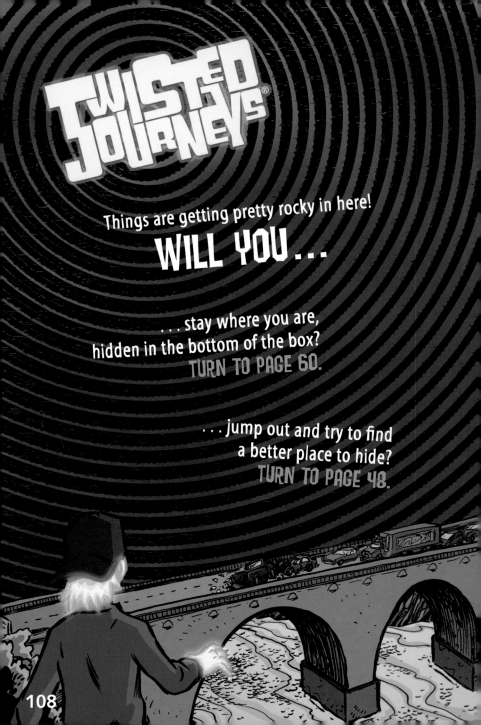

TWISTED JOURNEYS®

Things are getting pretty rocky in here!

WILL YOU...

. . . stay where you are,
hidden in the bottom of the box?
TURN TO PAGE 60.

. . . jump out and try to find
a better place to hide?
TURN TO PAGE 48.

You may not know much about quantum physics, but you're not convinced regular science will have much of an effect on your condition. "I think I'll go with Sergeant Fong on this one," you tell Major Green.

"Good choice," she tells you. "Fong was first in her class at MIT." She opens the door to the test chamber and lets you walk inside.

"Okay, ready when you are," you shout. Major Green closes the door, and lights start flashing on the walls around you. "Envision yourself growing," Green says through a speaker. "Like a sapling becoming a mighty oak."

You try to do what Green says . . . imagining the growing tree . . . and suddenly you *are* growing! It only takes a few seconds before you're back to your normal size!

Then you realize: You've grown right out of your clothes! Forget getting stepped on. Now you have to try not to die of embarrassment!

THE END

You figure you're better off trusting good, old-fashioned, reliable science than some weird idea that might not even work. "I'll go with Alpha, ma'am," you tell Major Green.

"Sounds good." She picks you up and sets you gently under the beam projectors. "Ready when you are, Sanderson."

The lab tech nods and starts counting down. "Three . . . two . . . one . . . now." He hits a switch and everything turns green . . .

. . . and then you're *shrinking again!* The world was already huge, but now it gets *enormous* . . . and then suddenly you're falling . . .

. . . because you're so tiny, you're starting to drop through the molecules of the machine you were standing on! And then you start shrinking faster and faster. You can't even process what your eyes are seeing, as you shrink to subatomic size . . .

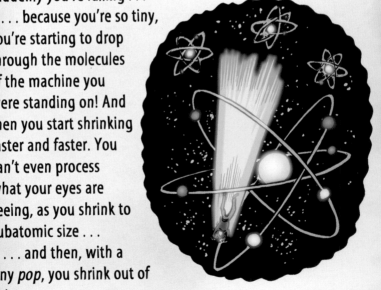

. . . and then, with a tiny *pop*, you shrink out of existence.

Your last thought is, "Way to go, Sanderson."

THE END

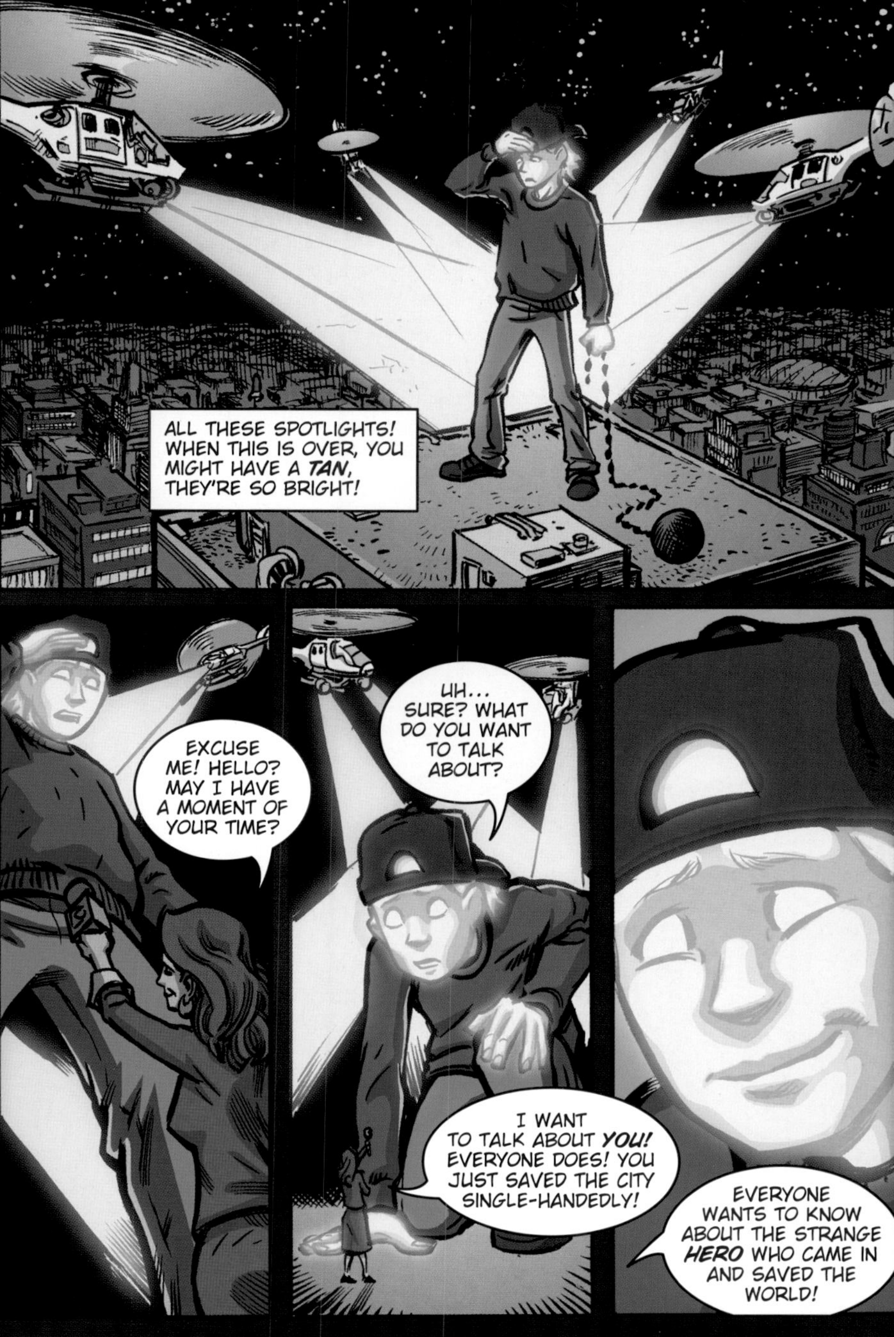
ALL THESE SPOTLIGHTS! WHEN THIS IS OVER, YOU MIGHT HAVE A *TAN*, THEY'RE SO BRIGHT!
EXCUSE ME! HELLO? MAY I HAVE A MOMENT OF YOUR TIME?
UH... SURE? WHAT DO YOU WANT TO TALK ABOUT?
I WANT TO TALK ABOUT *YOU!* EVERYONE DOES! YOU JUST SAVED THE CITY SINGLE-HANDEDLY!
EVERYONE WANTS TO KNOW ABOUT THE STRANGE *HERO* WHO CAME IN AND SAVED THE WORLD!

TURN TO PAGE 57.

WHICH TWISTED JOURNEYS® WILL YOU TRY NEXT?

#1 CAPTURED BY PIRATES
Will these scurvy pirates turn you into shark bait?

#2 ESCAPE FROM PYRAMID X
Not every ancient mummy stays dead . . .

#3 TERROR IN GHOST MANSION
The spooks in this Halloween house aren't wearing costumes . . .

#4 THE TREASURE OF MOUNT FATE
Can you survive monsters and magic and bring home the treasure?

#5 NIGHTMARE ON ZOMBIE ISLAND
Will you be the first to escape Zombie Island?

#6 THE TIME TRAVEL TRAP
Danger is everywhere when you're caught in a time machine!

#7 VAMPIRE HUNT
These vampire hunters are hunting for *you*!

#8 ALIEN INCIDENT ON PLANET J
Make peace with the aliens, or you'll never get off their planet . . .

#9 AGENT MONGOOSE AND THE HYPNO-BEAM SCHEME
Your top-secret mission: foil the plots of an evil mastermind!

#10 THE GOBLIN KING
Will you join the fearsome goblins or the dangerous elves?

#11 SHIPWRECKED ON MAD ISLAND
Mad scientists and mutants are on your trail!

#12 KUNG FU MASTERS
Can you master kung fu in time to battle bandits and ghosts?

#13 SCHOOL OF EVIL
The teachers are creepy, monsters lurk in the lab, and your dorm room is haunted!

#14 ATTACK OF THE MUTANT METEORS
Mysterious mayhem-making meteors could turn you as small as a bug or as tall as a skyscraper.

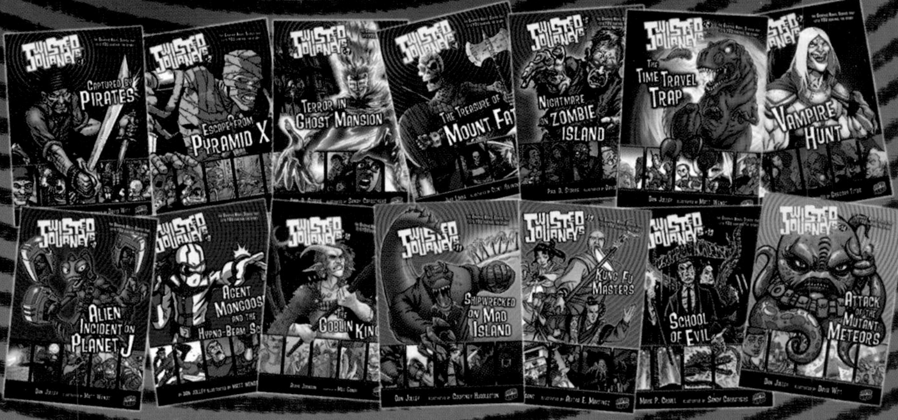

Captured by Pirates
Escape from Pyramid X
Terror in Ghost Mansion
The Treasure of Mount Fat
Nightmare on Zombie Island
The Time Travel Trap
Vampire Hunt
Alien Incident on Planet J
Agent Mongoose and the Hypno-Beam Sc
The Goblin Kin
Shipwrecked on Mad Island
Kung Fu Masters
School of Evil
Attack of the Mutant Meteors